A Grieving Embrace

The Cage She Left Behind

T.V. Snowden Jr

Published by 393 Media Group LLC

This is a work of fiction. Names, characters, places, and incidents are either the product of the author's imagination or are used fictitiously. Any resemblance to actual persons, living or dead, events, or locales is entirely coincidental.

Printed in the United States of America

ISBN: 979-8-9955743-0-9

ACKNOWLEDGEMENT

This story is about a man willing to tear the world apart to protect the people he loves. It is a story of survival, of fortresses, and of the light that finally breaks through the dark. I could not have written a single word of it without the people who served as my own foundation.

To my Dad: You are the architect of the man I am today. Thank you for your steady leadership and for the quiet, powerful guidance that defined my path. You didn't just tell me how to be a responsible man; you showed me. You taught me that a man's true strength isn't measured by what he takes, but by what he protects. I carry your lessons in every room I walk into.

To my Mom: Thank you for giving me the vision to see past the horizon. You were the one who taught me to never, ever accept "I can't" as an answer. Your unshakable faith in me—even during the seasons when I didn't have it in myself—is the reason I had the courage to finish this book. You taught me that with faith, no cage is permanent.

To my daughters: You are my greatest pride. Watching you chase your dreams with such fearlessness and grace is the most rewarding experience of my life. Every time I see you succeed, I am reminded of why I work as hard as I do. Never stop reaching. The world is yours, and I will always be in the front row, cheering the loudest.

To my son: You are only eight years old, but you carry a light that keeps me grounded. Every move I make, every story I tell, and every legacy I build is for you. My greatest prayer is to be the father you want and the man you truly need. I want you to look at my life and know that anything is possible if you have the heart to pursue it. You are my "why."

CONTENTS

Act I: The Fragile Foundation

1 The Collision 1

2 The Architect 8

3 The Echoes of the Cage 13

4 The Price of the Dark 21

5 I Am Home 27

6 The Yellow Room 32

7 The Heartbeat 36

8 The Anchor 41

9 The Burial 46

10 The Glass House 51

11 The Catalyst 58

12 The Fallout 63

Act II: The Descent & The Hunt

13	The Suffocation	70
14	The Extractor	74
15	The Descent	78
16	The Unearthing	83
17	The Catalyst for the Hunt	89
18	The Dead End	96
19	The Paper Trail	100
20	The Threshold	104
21	The Edge of the Map	108
22	Inside the Cage	113
23	The Extraction	118
24	The Michigamee Hunt	123

Act III: The Dual Labyrinth

25 Into the Maze 128

26 The Hallway of Doors 132

27 The Choke Point 137

28 The Ascent 142

29 The Interception 146

30 The Wreckage 150

31 The Cost of Freedom 155

Back Matter

32 The Light (Epilogue) 160

Call to Action (CTA) 164

EPIGRAPH

"...a lifelong, non-linear journey of integrating love and loss, rather than 'moving on' from pain. It involves navigating intense emotions to find resilience, transforming sorrow into a new way of living, and ultimately honoring the departed by carrying their memory forward." > — Unknown Author

ACT I: THE FRAGILE FOUNDATION

1 THE COLLISION

CHLOE

The world is entirely too loud, and it is entirely too fast. I sit at a small, scarred wooden table in the back corner of a crowded coffee shop. My hands wrap so tightly around a ceramic mug that the knuckles ache.

The coffee went cold at least twenty minutes ago, forming a dark, bitter film on the surface, but I don’t care. The mug gives my hands something to do other than shake. Most people come to coffee shops to work, to read, or to catch up with friends, completely oblivious to the fragility of the space around them.

I come here to practice pretending to be a human being. I press my back firmly against the exposed, cold brick wall. It isn't a preference; it is a strict tactical choice.

Rule number two of surviving the dark: never let anyone walk behind you. I methodically sweep the room, cataloging the threats with frantic, exhausting precision. Two exits. The front door with the annoying, high-pitched brass bell, and the solid metal fire door down the narrow hallway near the restrooms.

Sixteen patrons. Three of them are men wearing rugged winter boots. Every time one of those thick rubber soles strikes the hardwood floor, a phantom vibration echoes straight up the spine.

Muscles coil so tight they burn, bracing for a hand that isn't there, waiting to be dragged backward into a past I can't outrun. I take a slow, deliberate breath, trying to force the copper taste of adrenaline out of my mouth.

The hiss of the espresso machine is a snake in the grass. The overlapping chatter of the college students at the next table is television static cranked to maximum volume. Sensory overload.

I look up at the wall opposite my table to ground myself. Hanging there, illuminated by a warm track light, is a small canvas I painted—a chaotic, abstract storm of deep, bruising blues and thick, violent charcoal strokes. The café owner likes to showcase local artists, and after months of his gentle prodding, I finally relented.

It is the first time in my life I have ever let a piece of my mind be viewed by the public. An x-ray of a fractured ribcage, hung on the wall for tourists to gawk at. The brass bell above the front door jingles.

The body locks into a state of absolute paralysis. A man walks in. He is tall, with broad, commanding shoulders that immediately consume the narrow walkway between the crowded tables.

He wears a thick, dark cedar-colored winter coat that makes him look even larger, the collar turned up against the biting winter wind. A man that large can block an exit. A man that large can hold you down.

The sheer mass of him should send the heart rate into a dangerous, erratic sprint. But it doesn't. There is something fundamentally different about the way he moves.

He doesn't carry the suffocating gravity of a predator looking for weakness. His posture is relaxed, his dark eyes scanning the room with a quiet, patient intelligence. He doesn't stomp; he walks with a steady, deliberate grace that feels entirely unthreatening.

He orders a black coffee at the counter, pays, and turns around. His eyes land on the canvas hanging on the wall. He stops dead in his tracks.

I hold my breath, watching him from the safety of my corner. People usually glance at the art, feel a flicker of discomfort at the raw emotion bleeding off the canvas, and quickly move on. But he doesn't move on.

He actually looks at it. He studies the violent charcoal strokes as if deciphering a map left behind by a shipwreck survivor. Then, his gaze shifts.

He looks away from the painting and looks directly across the room. At me. He knows.

Somehow, just by looking at the jagged lines I drew, his analytical brain instantly connects the chaos on the wall to the girl shrinking into the brickwork in the corner. He starts walking toward my table. The chest tightens, the air trapping itself in the lungs.

Exit strategy, the brain screams. He's too big. You can't fight him.

Drop the mug, flip the table to slow him down, and run for the fire door. But before the panic can fully articulate itself, he stops. He stays a polite, respectful distance from the edge of my table.

He doesn't loom over me, and he doesn't cast a shadow over my space. He keeps his hands out of his pockets, resting casually at his sides, entirely visible.

"It's loud," he says. His voice is a deep, grounding rumble.

It doesn't add to the chaotic noise of the café; it instantly cuts right through it, dropping an anchor into the frantic ocean of the mind. I blink, completely off guard. "Excuse me?"

He gestures with a slight nod to the painting on the wall. "The painting. It's incredibly beautiful, but it's incredibly loud. Like someone screaming underwater."

He looks back down at me, his dark eyes entirely sincere. "I'm Alex."

"Chloe," I whisper. The name feels fragile and dusty in the throat, like a word not used in years.

He offers a small, easy smile. He doesn't ask to sit down. He doesn't push into my boundary.

"It's nice to meet you, Chloe. You have an incredible—"

CRASH. A barista near the counter drops a plastic bus tub full of dirty ceramic mugs. The sharp, violent sound of shattering porcelain explodes through the small café like a gunshot.

I flinch violently. Shoulders instantly hunch toward the ears. Hands fly up to protect the back of the head, knocking the cold coffee over.

It spills across the table, but I don't care. I slam my eyes shut, bracing for the inevitable strike. In a fraction of a second, the coffee shop vanishes.

The linoleum floor returns. The smell of damp wood fills the air. Waiting for the thudding boots.

Waiting for the calloused hand to twist into the hair. Waiting for the pain. But the pain doesn't come.

I force my eyes open. The heart hammers a frantic, terrifying rhythm against the ribs, a cold sweat breaking out across the back of the neck. Alex doesn't ask what is wrong.

He doesn't stare like I am broken, crazy, or dangerous. He doesn't draw the attention of the staring patrons to the panic attack. Instead, he simply takes a half-step to his left.

He positions his broad shoulders perfectly between me and the chaos of the broken mugs. He blocks the sightline of the whispering college students. He becomes a physical, impenetrable wall, casting a long, safe shadow over my table, giving me the crucial, private seconds needed to remember how to breathe.

He looks down at me, his expression perfectly calm, as if dropping into a defensive stance to protect a stranger is the most natural thing in the world.

"They need a better system for those mugs," he says mildly, his voice steady and completely unbothered by the chaos behind him. He is giving me an out. He is giving me my dignity back.

I let my hands slowly drop to the table. The frantic pounding in the chest begins to ease, entirely neutralized by the steady, unmovable presence of the man standing in front of me. For the first time in fourteen years, I am looking at a man whose size could easily destroy me, and I don't see a monster.

I see a safe harbor…

Forty minutes later, I stand alone in the hallway of my apartment building. The warmth from the coffee shop is completely gone, evaporating into the frigid evening air the second I walked away from him. The walk home through the city streets is a cold reminder of reality.

I slide my key into the bottom lock of my door and turn it. Then the middle deadbolt. Then the thick, reinforced chain lock at the top.

I push the door open, step inside the dark apartment, and immediately engage all three locks again, plunging my life back into a profound, suffocating silence. I walk straight into the bathroom and flick on the harsh overhead vanity light.

I stare at the woman in the mirror. She looks completely exhausted. The dark circles under her eyes are bruised and heavy.

She looks like someone who just spent an hour pretending she isn't shattered into a million jagged pieces. I open the medicine cabinet. Pushed all the way to the back, hidden behind a box of bandages and a spare tube of toothpaste, is a small, amber prescription bottle.

Zolpidem. I don't open it. I just reach out and wrap my trembling fingers around the plastic cylinder, letting the chemical promise of a dreamless sleep anchor me to the tile floor.

Alex looked at me like I was a puzzle he actually wanted to solve. He looked at me like I was something worth protecting. But he doesn't know the truth.

He doesn't know that the girl he shielded in the coffee shop is a walking ghost. He doesn't know about the velvet box hidden beneath my mattress, or the tiny, yellowed infant's sock locked inside of it. I squeeze the plastic bottle, the hard plastic edges digging painfully into the palm.

You can't let him in, the dark, familiar voice in the head whispers, smelling faintly of scorched grease and damp cedar. Rule number one. Stay hidden.

Be quiet. If you let him in, the past will destroy him, too. I let go of the bottle, shut the cabinet door, and turn off the light, entirely surrendering to the dark.

2 THE ARCHITECT

ALEX

Alex was a man who managed risk for a living. Sitting at the solid oak desk in the study of his suburban home, he stared blankly at the glowing screen of his laptop. The house was completely silent, save for the low, rhythmic hum of the central heating fighting off the bitter Michigan winter outside. In his line of work—managing complex product lifecycles—he was paid handsomely to identify vulnerabilities, mitigate disasters, and keep highly volatile variables strictly controlled. With his years of managing scaled, high-stakes roadmaps, his entire worldview was structured around predictable sprints and measurable outcomes. He built frameworks. He cleared blockers. He fixed things.

But for the last forty-eight hours, his highly analytical brain had been completely derailed by a variable he couldn't solve: the girl from the coffee shop. He hadn't been able to stop thinking about the way she looked right before the ceramic mugs had shattered. Chloe. She had been sitting with her back pressed flush against the brick wall, her dark, haunted eyes tracking every single patron in the room with the hyper-vigilant precision of a soldier navigating a minefield. And when the crash happened, she hadn't just startled like a normal person caught off guard by a loud noise. She had physically braced for a violent, physical impact that only she could see.

Alex tapped his weighted silver pen against the mahogany desk, the rhythmic clicking filling the quiet room. He opened a new tab on his browser, his fingers resting over the keyboard. He just wanted to send her flowers. Maybe buy the chaotic, beautifully violent charcoal piece she had painted. It was a simple, normal, socially acceptable impulse. He typed her first name and the name of the coffee shop into the search bar and hit enter. Nothing.

He searched the local Detroit art gallery registries, filtering by recent exhibitions and emerging Midtown artists. Nothing. He expanded the search parameters to social media platforms, running reverse image searches on the types of abstract art she painted and cross-referencing local artist tags. Zero results. Alex leaned back in his leather chair, the harsh blue glow of the monitor illuminating the deep, frustrated furrow in his brow.

In the modern world, it was almost mathematically impossible to exist without leaving a digital footprint. You didn't just casually avoid the internet; you had to actively, obsessively scrub yourself from the grid to achieve this level of anonymity. He thought back to the brief interaction at her table. She hadn't had a smartphone sitting next to her coffee mug. When he had watched her leave from the frosted window of the café, he had noticed she paid the barista in exact paper cash, leaving no credit card trail. All the warning systems in Alex's risk-averse brain began to ring in perfect, deafening unison.

The absence of data was the data. People who pay strictly in cash, systematically avoid digital footprints, and map the fire exits of a room aren't just eccentric, introverted artists. They are ghosts. And people only become ghosts when they are running from something utterly terrifying. Logic dictated that he should close the laptop. As a man who spent his life analyzing risk versus reward, the mandate was clear: flag this as a critical warning, abandon the pursuit, and stick to the safe, predictable parameters of his meticulously organized life.

Instead, Alex abruptly closed the browser, grabbed his thick cedar coat off the back of the chair, and headed for the front door. The mystery wasn't a deterrent; it was a gravitational pull he couldn't fight. He spent the next three afternoons working remotely from that exact same Midtown coffee shop. He sat at a table near the front, nursing black coffee, answering emails on his phone, and waiting. On the fourth day, just as the afternoon light began to fade into a bruised purple dusk, the brass bell jingled, and she walked in.

She looked just as fragile and tightly coiled as the first time he had seen her. She was wrapped in a thick, oversized knit scarf that seemed to swallow her small frame entirely. Alex didn't rush her. He knew better than to corner an animal that was already looking for a trap. He waited until she had secured her corner table, keeping her back firmly to the brick wall, before he pushed his chair back and approached. He kept his hands completely out of his pockets. He moved slowly, deliberately broadcasting his intentions.

"I didn't think I'd see you again," Chloe said softly as he stopped a few feet away. She didn't smile, but she didn't flinch, either. Her dark eyes immediately darted to his hands, then to the door behind him, before finally settling on his face.

"I was hoping you would," Alex said, intentionally keeping his voice in that low, steady register. "I'd like to take you to dinner, Chloe. Somewhere quiet."

He saw the immediate, visceral panic flare in her eyes. He could practically see the gears turning violently in her head, calculating the immense risk of letting a stranger into her carefully constructed fortress. Her knuckles turned white as she gripped the edge of the wooden table.

"I don't... I don't do well in crowds," she deflected, her voice thin and breathy.

"Then we won't go to a crowd," Alex countered smoothly, anticipating the blocker and offering an immediate solution. "Belle Isle Conservatory. It's wide open, the ceilings are entirely glass, and it's completely empty on a Tuesday evening. Just walking. No pressure. No enclosed spaces."

He watched her process the parameters. Open space. High visibility. Easy exits. He was speaking her language of survival without her even realizing he knew the dialect. Slowly, almost imperceptibly, the rigid tension in her jaw eased. She took a shallow breath and gave a single, tight nod. "Okay."

An hour later, Alex parked his SUV near the entrance of the Belle Isle Conservatory. The heavy doors of the greenhouse opened, offering an immediate, stark contrast to the bitter, grey Detroit winter outside. It was a sprawling, humid sanctuary of vibrant green, wrapped in an immense dome of curved glass that let the fading evening light pour in. The air was dense, and smelled richly of damp earth, blooming orchids, and wet stone. They walked side-by-side down the paved brick pathways. Alex maintained a careful, measured distance.

He didn't try to touch her arm to guide her, and he didn't brush her hand. He let her set the exact pace, giving her total autonomy over the physical space between them. As she talked—quietly, guardedly—about her charcoal sketches and her deep love for the way harsh shadows manipulated light, Alex didn't just listen; he studied her. He looked past the beautiful slope of her nose and the dark, expressive eyes. He saw the profound, bone-deep exhaustion hiding just beneath the surface of her brown skin.

He noticed the way her eyes constantly, involuntarily tracked the single, bored security guard patrolling the far end of the fern room. He saw the way she instinctively adjusted her stride to ensure she was always positioned between Alex and the nearest glass exit door. She wasn't just guarded. She was a fortress under active siege. *She's broken*, his analytical mind whispered, the reality of the situation finally setting in. Whatever she is running from is immense. It is violent. And it is still chasing her.

Alex stopped walking. Chloe took two more steps before realizing the sound of his footsteps had ceased. She turned back to look at him, her dark eyes wide, questioning, and instantly defensive. The artificial sunset lighting of the conservatory caught the edge of her face, illuminating the stark terror hiding just behind her artistic mask. She looked incredibly beautiful, and incredibly, tragically lost.

In that quiet, humid second, surrounded by towering palms and absolute silence, the risk-manager in Alex completely surrendered to the protector. He didn't care about the missing digital footprint anymore. He didn't care about the cash payments, the hyper-vigilance, or the sheer, undeniable danger of attaching himself to a ghost. He looked at the fragile, terrified woman standing in front of him, and he made a silent, unbreakable vow.

Whatever chased you into the dark, Alex thought, his jaw setting with an absolute, unshakeable resolve, *I am going to build a wall it can never break through. I am going to be your anchor. I will never let it touch you here.* He offered her a small, reassuring smile, asking no questions, demanding no answers, and simply took a step forward to join her on the path. He was completely, tragically unaware of the absolute monster he had just challenged to a war.

3 THE ECHOES OF THE CAGE

CHLOE

The slow, hypnotic rhythm of the ceiling fan offers absolutely no peace. I lie flat on my back in the center of the mattress, eyes wide open, staring up at the spinning wooden blades as they chop the ambient streetlight into rhythmic, dizzying slices of shadow across the ceiling.

I roll over. My hand instinctively reaches out for the left side of the bed. Fingers graze the cold, undisturbed cotton of the fitted sheet.

The body flinches back instantly, snatching the hand away, pressing it to the chest as if the soft fabric burns. Sleep is a luxury reserved strictly for people with quiet minds. Mine is currently a riot.

I push myself up against the headboard, the movement is weary and deeply practiced. On my nightstand, illuminated by the harsh orange glow of a streetlamp filtering through the blinds, sit the two absolute anchors of my nocturnal existence: an amber prescription bottle of Zolpidem and my worn, thick leather-bound journal.

I pick up the bottle. The plastic rattles loudly in the profound silence of the apartment. I shake a single white pill into my palm and swallow it dry.

It scrapes down the throat—a harsh, physical reminder that I am here, completely alone behind three deadbolts, and the grounding warmth of Alex's presence is miles away. I pick up my pen and crack the journal open. The handwriting is jagged, frantic, pressed so hard into the paper it nearly tears the page as it scores the lines.

5,110 days. The silence is still the loudest thing in this house. It's in these quiet, isolated moments—between the hours of three and four in the morning—that her absence is most pronounced.

The echoes of sorrow don't ever actually fade. They just change pitch, settling deep into the bones until you forget what it feels like to live without the ache. I close the book, toss the pen onto the nightstand, and stand up.

I walk across the cold hardwood floor to the bathroom mirror. The woman looking back seems dangerously dim in this light, entirely stripped of the vibrant, artistic energy Alex pulled out of me just hours ago at the conservatory.

I reach up with my right hand and aggressively rub the spot on my opposite wrist where a faint, stubborn smudge of cadmium red paint remains. I scrubbed it with turpentine the second I got home, trying to erase the memory of the canvas from the skin, but it clings to the pores like dried blood.

The canvas has to be clean. I have to be clean. I abandon the mirror and move to the living room window, leaning my forehead against the freezing glass pane.

Outside, the city skyline sprawls out before me—an immense, indifferent grid of static yellow streetlights and deep, concrete shadows. Breath fogs the glass, obscuring the world outside.

"Just... shut up," I whisper to the empty room, my voice cracking. "Please." I let my eyes drift closed.

The shocking, icy sensation of the glass against the skin sends a violent shiver down the spine, and suddenly, the sprawling city completely disappears. The air in the lungs grows incredibly dense. It tastes like metallic dust, smelling strongly of scorched grease and rotting, damp wood.

Not in the high-rise apartment anymore. Swallowed up by a thin, moth-eaten quilt in a childhood bedroom. The flickering, dying bulb of a bedside lamp casts long, wrapping shadows that dance like starving monsters against the peeling, water-damaged floral wallpaper.

Total paralysis. Beneath the covers, small hands grip the edges of the mattress so tightly the knuckles ache. Lungs refuse to expand.

If a breath is taken, he will hear it. In the corner of the room, seated in a high-backed wooden chair, is a figure. Facing away, perfectly, terrifyingly still.

The dim, sickly light catches the stiff fabric of his broad shoulder and the thick leather of his boots. A high, thin whimper escapes the throat. Unstoppable.

The sound of pure, concentrated terror. The figure hears it. He stands abruptly.

The solid wooden legs of the chair scrape violently against the floorboards—a sound that vibrates straight through the teeth. He turns slowly. The flickering lamplight catches the lower half of his face, illuminating a cruel, tight smirk.

He takes a single, deliberate, earth-shaking step toward the bed. A gasp. Eyes snap open.

I rip myself away from the cold glass of the window, the chest heaving as the sterile, modern light of the apartment rushes back in. A ghost haunting its own home, framed by a vast, suffocating emptiness. Trembling uncontrollably, I walk back to the bedroom and drop to my knees beside the bed.

I reach deep under the mattress, my arm scraping against the box spring. My fingers find the small, wooden box hidden in the darkest corner. I pull it out and sit on the floor, breath hitching as the mechanical brass latch clicks loudly in the quiet room.

Inside, nestled on a bed of dark, faded velvet, is a tiny infant's sock. The aged, yellowed cotton looks impossibly fragile under the harsh bedroom light. A stylized letter "T" is carefully embroidered on the ankle in faded pink thread.

My thumb traces the shape of the letter. The haunting expression of the little girl in the nightmare—the child left behind in that house—stares back from the absolute depths of memory.

I wish I'd fought for you, the thought forms, the familiar, crushing weight of guilt settling over the ribs like a lead apron. *I wish I had been strong enough to take you with me.* But I just ran... I was a coward.

And now, it is five thousand, one hundred and ten days too late. I snap the wooden box shut, shove it back under the mattress, and crawl into bed. The mattress deforms under my weight, trapping me in the center.

I stare up at the ceiling fan again. On the nightstand, the digital alarm clock flips forward with a mechanical, aggressive sound. Tick... Tick... Tick...

"Move," I whisper, a dry, raspy plea to the glowing red numbers. "Please. Just move."

Time doesn't actually heal all wounds. It just mocks you. It drags its feet because it knows you're waiting for a morning that never actually feels like a new start.

My hand begins to tap frantically against the duvet, drumming a rapid, erratic rhythm to fight off the suffocating quiet. I pull the thick covers all the way up to my chin, making myself as small as physically possible, bracing to fight the shadows until dawn. But the ticking of the alarm clock isn't just a sound anymore; it is a physical, crushing blow to the sternum.

Thud... Thud... Thud... Not a clock. Footsteps.

In the mind, the hands of the clock begin to spin at an impossible, dizzying speed, dragging violently backward through time. The sterile, cool, climate-controlled air of the apartment vanishes entirely, instantly replaced by the stifling dread of the house in Michigamee County. Back in the hallway.

Looking down at trembling, impossibly young hands. A chaotic heartbeat hammers in the throat while frantically shoving clothes and a handful of cash into a pillowcase. Got to get out.

Got to run. Then, the floorboards groan. A thick, suffocating silhouette completely blocks the dim light from the stairwell, swallowing the narrow hallway in absolute dread.

I bolt. A blur of frantic motion, bare feet scrambling for traction against the slick wood. But not fast enough.

A brutal, calloused hand lunges out of the dark. It tangles viciously in the back of the hair, yanking backward with a force that nearly snaps the neck. A sickening crack against the floor reverberates straight through the skull, stunning the brain.

Being dragged. Friction burns the skin like fire. Fingers frantically claw and score at the floorboards, nails bending backward and splintering, leaving stark white streaks on the wood.

The mouth opens, a jagged, blood-curdling scream tearing up the throat, but the sound is violently suffocated by the absolute, crushing black of the hallway. Eyes snap open. Gasping for air, the chest heaves violently against the duvet of the present-day bed.

Not just lying there; the entire body is completely rigid, the jaw locked so tight the back teeth ache. Drenched in a freezing, clammy sweat. Breathing slow and deliberate—the terrified, hyper-vigilant rhythm of a soldier hunkered down in a foxhole waiting for the artillery to hit.

Fighting the border of reality, doing everything in physical power to keep the shadows from dragging back under. I turn my head. The moonlight catches the edge of my phone sitting on the nightstand next to the pills.

My hand twitches on the covers. A sick, exhausted, desperate part of the brain just wants to surrender. Wants to swallow the rest of the Zolpidem, turn off the lights, and let the dark finally take over.

No. Defiance is the only thing keeping the mind from disappearing completely. I take a sharp, jagged breath, refusing to let the single tear caught in my lashes fall.

I need a lifeline. An anchor before the undertow hits again. I force my mind violently away from the dark and pivot toward the light.

I close my eyes and reach for the memory of him. Just a few nights ago. The living room a square of deep, quiet shadows.

Pacing the floor, stomach in absolute knots. Tossing the phone onto the sofa, a fragile whisper to the empty room: "Call. Just call."

As if conjured by the sheer force of longing, the phone vibrated against the cushion. Not just a buzz; a defibrillator to a flatlining heart. The screen reads: ALEX.

"Hello?" I answered, breath catching.

"I'm outside," his filtered voice replied, low, steady, and entirely undeniable.

The heart skipped a violent beat. Before the words could even be processed, a sharp, urgent knock rattled the front door. I sprinted across the room, throwing the deadbolts open.

Alex stood there in the hallway. Completely out of breath, looking at me like he was witnessing an absolute miracle. No waiting for an invitation, no hesitation.

He stepped inside, his broad shoulders consuming the space as he slammed the solid door shut against the rest of the world. "I tried to wait," he breathed, eyes dark and entirely focused. "I made it three blocks before I turned the car around."

He reached for me. His large hands found my waist, pulling me flush against the hard, warm wall of his chest. The exact opposite of the violent, calloused hands in the nightmares; this grip was a desperate, protective anchor.

I melted into him, winding my arms tightly around his neck, my fingers tangling in his hair. "I was waiting," I started to say. "I was—"

He cut me off with a kiss. Not tender, not cautious. A collision.

A total, intoxicating surrender. He lifted me. Instinctively, eagerly, I locked my legs around his waist.

As he carried me toward the bedroom, I buried my face in the collar of his coat, breathing in the scent of cedar and clean soap. In his arms, the ghosts couldn't reach. For the first time in my life, I finally let myself feel completely, wonderfully safe in the dark.

4 THE PRICE OF THE DARK

CHLOE

The clinical, blinding white light of the gallery bounces off the pristine walls, threatening to trigger a massive migraine right behind the eyes. I balance near the top of a sleek aluminum stepladder, meticulously adjusting the angle of an oversized canvas.

The air in the gallery smells of cold concrete, ozone from the track lighting, and the sharp, metallic tang of linseed oil. I am running on absolute fumes. Muscles ache with a deep, dragging exhaustion that the three cups of black coffee sitting on the curator's desk can't begin to touch.

I wipe the back of my hand across my cheek, leaving a smear of damp cobalt blue paint against brown skin. I take a shaky breath, staring at the canvas in front of me.

Six hours in this sterile white room, trying to arrange the chaotic pieces of my mind into something wealthy people want to hang in their dining rooms. It feels less like preparing for an art exhibition and more like setting up my own autopsy.

Suddenly, the loud brass door chime shrieks. Not a pleasant, welcoming ring. A sharp, metallic discord that slices right through the quiet room like a guillotine.

The body violently flinches. A foot slips an inch on the ladder rung. The heart immediately launches into a frantic, panicked sprint against the ribs, hammering so hard it rattles the teeth.

I grip the sides of the ladder, knuckles turning stark white, and force my eyes toward the entrance, the brain already mapping the distance to the fire exit in the back alley. Lila stands in the threshold. She doesn't just enter a room; she occupies it.

Dressed in a sharp, structured wool coat—pitch black and unapologetically expensive. Dark hair pulled back into a severe, flawless style. She moves across the polished concrete floor with a slow, deliberate grace.

The sharp click-clack of her heels echoes in the cavernous space. A predator assessing the nave of a white cathedral, searching for a pulse.

"Chloe," she murmurs, her sharp eyes scanning the room, taking in the dozen canvases leaning against the walls. "It's breathtaking. I can feel the energy in the room before I even step fully inside."

I slowly climb down the ladder, legs feel like lead. I grab a rag from my back pocket, aggressively wiping the cobalt blue from trembling hands.

I take a deep breath, forcing the heart rate to slow, and paste a brittle, practiced smile onto my face. The mask of the 'Professional Artist.' The version of me that isn't afraid of the dark.

"Lila," I breathe out, tossing the rag onto a nearby worktable. "I... I wasn't expecting you until tomorrow evening. The lighting isn't even set yet."

She ignores the greeting, drifting past me toward a sprawling, six-foot piece I titled *Feelings of Deafening Silence*. She stands perfectly still, staring at the thick, chaotic layers of ash grey and bruised purple.

The canvas is textured, built up with layers of acrylic and crushed charcoal scraped onto the fabric with a palette knife when the night terrors were too loud for sleep. "A bold title," Lila says, her voice dropping an octave, reverent and hungry.

"It feels like a scream held underwater. What were you thinking about when you mixed these greys, Chloe? There's a desperation here. A feeling of being entirely trapped."

The throat tightens. Thinking about the smell of wet cedar. Thinking about the locks on the doors.

"Just... the noise of the city," I lie smoothly, the words tasting like ash. "The isolation of being surrounded by millions of people but feeling completely alone."

Lila tears her eyes away from the canvas and looks at me. She reaches out and places her hand firmly on my shoulder. I don't pull away, but the entire body goes instantly rigid.

When Alex touches me, his hands are a shield keeping the world out. His touch is a deep, grounding anchor. Lila's touch is entirely different.

Her grip is firm, static, and demanding—the touch of a miner assessing a vein of gold. She isn't trying to heal the pain; she is trying to extract the emotion right out of the skin to see how much it is worth.

"You've been gone a long time, Lila," I say, my voice barely above a whisper, desperate to change the subject. "I thought... maybe you'd moved on to other talent. You haven't checked in since the winter."

"Never." She turns to me, her dark eyes pinning me in place. Her thumb presses slightly into my collarbone.

"The world is a whirlwind, my dear. Artists come and go. But I always come back to the source."

"And you... you are the fire. You just need to let it burn." She lets her hand drop from my shoulder and glides toward the back of the gallery.

She stops in front of a newer piece, one I hadn't even planned on putting in the show. Visceral and entirely abstract—thick, jagged, violent strokes of cadmium red clashing against cold, dead, suffocating greys.

Painted in a manic haze at three in the morning, pouring every ounce of the silent terror from the nightmares straight onto the canvas. The closest I ever came to painting the monster's face.

"This one," Lila says, her breath catching slightly. Genuinely captivated. "My god, Chloe. It's raw. It's... bleeding."

She places a hand over her own heart, completely entranced by the pain manifested there. She steps closer to it, as if she wants to climb inside the chaos.

"Where did this come from?" she asks softly. "This isn't just city isolation. This is grief. This is a violent severing. Who hurt you this badly?"

I stand frozen in the center of the gallery. My thumb instinctively finds a spot of dried paint on my index finger. I begin to pick at it, scratching the edge of the cuticle over and over until the skin underneath is raw and burning.

The track lighting above suddenly feels like an interrogation lamp. The thought of strangers in expensive suits holding flutes of champagne, staring at this canvas, pointing at the nightmare, feels like being slowly peeled alive.

They will buy it because it looks edgy. They will hang it above modern fireplaces, completely unaware they are looking at a portrait of a kitchenette in Michigamee County. Looking at the suffocating guilt of a child left behind in the dark.

"It's just an exploration of color," I stammer, my voice cracking under the weight of the lie. "Don't bullshit me, Chloe," Lila says softly, never taking her eyes off the red paint.

"I know you. I know your work. This is a confession. What do you want for it?"

The stomach bottoms out. "Twelve thousand," I say, the number tumbling out of my mouth before I can stop it.

Blood money. Putting a price tag on the worst night of my life, selling the ghosts of the past just to keep the lights on and the deadbolts secured. A physical sickness settles in the gut.

"A steal," Lila whispers reverently. "I can feel the weight of it from here. You feel it too, don't you? The sorrow?"

"Every line," I nod, fighting the tears welling in my eyes. "It's a piece of her. Of everything I couldn't say."

I swallow hard, staring at the jagged red strokes, the image of the tiny, yellowed "T" sock flashing violently in the mind. "Sometimes it feels like it's pulling me under."

Lila takes a slow step away from the canvas and closes the distance between us. Her eyes gleam with a complex mix of maternal affection and ruthless, commercial hunger.

"Then let it pull you under," she urges softly, her voice dropping into a hypnotic cadence. "But let the world watch you drown. You can't keep this bottled up in your apartment forever."

"This is what makes you brilliant. An exhibition, Chloe. A real one. People need to see this fire. They need to see your scars."

I look up at her, completely defeated by her intensity. I am so incredibly tired. Tired of mapping exits.

Tired of locking doors. Tired of fighting the current of memory. A single tear breaks free, tracking a hot line right through the blue paint on my cheek.

"I'm taking this piece," Lila declares, her tone softening beautifully as she steps directly into my space. "I need it near me. And I'm sorry I haven't been here, Chloe. I shouldn't have left you to navigate this alone. Forgive me?"

Before I can answer, she pulls me into a tight, encompassing embrace. Commanding and demanding all at once. Not the safety of Alex.

The embrace of a woman who needs the pain to remain profitable. But the strength to hold the professional mask up for another second is completely gone.

I bury my face into the expensive, stiff wool of her shoulder, let out a broken, jagged exhale, and finally let myself cry. Weeping for the girl in the nightgown, weeping for the monster I am putting on display.

5 I AM HOME

CHLOE

The light in the bedroom isn't the harsh, sterile, neon glare of the city that usually bleeds through the apartment blinds. It is a soft, buttery gold, spilling rich and warm across the thick duvet.

I wake up slowly. For a fleeting, terrifying second, the body tenses out of pure, ingrained habit.

The mind automatically braces for the familiar, crushing weight of panic to settle over the chest. Waiting for the phantom smell of damp wood. Waiting for the lingering echo of Artie's thudding boots.

Waiting for the frantic, erratic hammering of the heart to signal that the nightmare has found me again. It doesn't come.

The heart beats in a slow, steady, incredibly calm rhythm. The jaw isn't clenched tight enough to crack the teeth. Fingers aren't dug into the mattress like claws.

For the first time in five thousand, one hundred and ten days, the nervous system is entirely quiet. I turn my head against the pillow.

The space beside me is empty, the sheets tangled and still holding the deep, radiating heat of his body. The quiet in this room isn't a threat.

It isn't the profound, stifling silence of the deadbolted apartment, where quiet just means the monsters are hiding. This quiet is a deep, exhausted exhale. It is peace.

I sit up, the cool morning air brushing across bare shoulders. I look around the room.

It is distinctly Alex—immaculately clean, structured, and grounded by solid, dark wood furniture. No chaotic piles of canvases, no manic charcoal sketches scattered across the floor. A room built for rest, not for survival.

Draped over the edge of a deep velvet armchair in the corner is the crisp, white button-down shirt Alex wore to the gallery the night before. I slide out of the expansive bed, bare feet sinking into the plush rug, and walk over to the chair.

I reach out and slip the shirt on. The thick cotton is cool against the skin but instantly comforting, swallowing my small frame entirely. The hem falls halfway down my thighs.

Not just a piece of clothing; a physical layer of armor. I roll the sleeves up past my elbows and instinctively bury my nose in the stiff collar.

It smells of sharp cedar, expensive soap, and the intense, intoxicating heat of his skin. It smells exactly like safety.

I wrap my arms around my waist, pulling the fabric tighter against me, and let out a long breath. I pad barefoot out of the bedroom and down the wide hallway, following the rich, dark aroma of roasted coffee beans.

The kitchen is spacious, with polished granite counters and large windows flooding the space with brilliant, unfiltered sunlight. Alex stands by the island, his back to me, expertly working a large, stainless steel espresso machine.

He wears low-slung grey sweatpants and a plain, fitted black t-shirt that stretches tightly across the broad expanse of his shoulders as he moves. I stop in the doorway and lean against the wooden frame, crossing my arms over my chest, and just watch him.

The hyper-vigilant, terrified woman who constantly scans rooms for fire exits and maps out defensive escape routes is completely gone. Today, the artist in me just wants to stand in the quiet and memorize the exact way the morning light catches the sharp, masculine edge of his jaw.

To paint the effortless, grounded way he takes up space in the room. He must feel the subtle shift in the air, or maybe he just possesses a sixth sense when it comes to me.

He turns around, holding two steaming ceramic mugs, and stops dead in his tracks. The casual, easy grace he usually carries himself with vanishes for a split second.

His dark eyes track from the oversized collar of his shirt draped over my shoulders, down the line of my bare legs, and back up to my face. He looks completely, beautifully undone—like a man who spent his entire life building rigid, predictable corporate structures, only to realize this messy, quiet morning is the only thing he actually wants to keep.

"I was going to say good morning," he murmurs, his voice low, intimate, and gravelly with sleep. "But I think you just ruined me for all other mornings."

A sudden, unfamiliar heat rises to my cheeks, completely disarming the emotional defenses I usually carry. I don't want to hide from him. I don't want to build a wall.

"I commandeered your shirt," I say softly, stepping fully into the sunlight of the kitchen. "I hope you don't mind. My clothes from last night smelled like oil paint and panic."

"Keep it," he says without a second of hesitation. His gaze drops to my lips as he walks across the kitchen to meet me. He presses a warm mug into my hands. "You wear it infinitely better than I do. It's officially yours."

He doesn't step back after handing over the coffee. He stays close, his physical proximity acting as a warm gravitational pull.

He reaches up, his large, calloused thumb gently brushing a stray lock of dark hair behind my ear. The touch is so tender, so completely devoid of demands or expectations, that it makes the chest physically ache.

He leans down, pressing a soft, lingering kiss to my temple. I close my eyes, leaning into the pressure of his lips, the chest brushing lightly against his before he finally turns back to the refrigerator to grab the cream.

I take a sip of the coffee—it is dark, rich, and perfect—and walk over to the sturdy oak dining table sitting in the alcove of the kitchen. My worn, leather-bound journal, the one I carry everywhere like a defensive shield, sits on the edge of the table where it spilled out of my tote bag the night before.

I set my mug down on a coaster and slowly flip the thick cover open. I stare down at the pages. Usually, this book is an absolute graveyard.

The pages are filled with jagged, frantic handwriting, tallying the thousands of days of silence. A map of the nightmares I can't outrun, filled with dark, desperate poetry about the child left behind in the cold.

To write something good in this book feels incredibly dangerous. Daring the universe to notice the happiness and violently snatch it away.

I pick up the pen resting in the spine. My hand hovers over a blank, crisp white page. The pulse flutters nervously in the throat.

I look up. Alex leans against the granite counter, blowing softly on his dark coffee. He isn't checking his phone. He isn't looking out the window.

He is just watching me with an expression of such pure, uncomplicated, unwavering devotion that it completely shatters the last remaining lock on the heart. I swallow the dense, metallic lump of fear in the throat, looking back down at the blank page.

The ink flows smooth, deliberate, and entirely unafraid. I am home. I stare at the three words.

They feel monumental. To anyone else, just a fleeting, romantic thought written on a Sunday morning. But to a woman who has spent five thousand, one hundred and ten days feeling like a terrified ghost haunting her own life, it is a terrifying, beautiful, total surrender.

I close the journal, running my fingertips gently over the worn leather cover. For the first time in fourteen years, the monster in the dark is finally quiet. I actually believe I am safe.

6 THE YELLOW ROOM

ALEX

Alex was a man who found his peace in structure. He stood near the center of the spare bedroom, balanced on a sleek aluminum step ladder. The air in the quiet room was dense, thick with the sharp, metallic smell of latex paint and the faintly sweet ozone scent of the track lighting. He dipped a fine-tipped trim brush into a plastic tray of warm, pale-yellow paint and meticulously cut in along the ceiling line, pulling a perfect, unmoving edge against the blue painter's tape he had spent three hours applying the night before. He liked things measured. He liked things secure.

In a world that had been chaotic and terrifying for the woman he loved, he took immense pride in building a physical sanctuary where the variables were finally controlled. He looked around the room, which, just three days prior, had been a barren storage crypt filled with flat-packed furniture and the ghosts of projects never started. Now, it was a safe haven in progress. A lot can happen in twelve months. It had been one year since he had shielded a terrified, nameless girl from a pile of shattered ceramic mugs in a Midtown coffee shop. A year since they had walked the wide-open, glass-domed pathways of the Belle Isle Conservatory. A year since he had seen her completely raw and shattered, only to hold her through the night and watch her write *I am home* in a journal that usually read like a casualty report.

Alex dipped his brush again, moving down the ladder. Their new house, nestled on a quiet, tree-lined street in the Detroit suburbs, was miles away from the heavily deadbolted high-rise where she had been living. When they moved in, Alex had personally installed a top-tier, integrated smart security system with 360-degree cameras and glass-break sensors. But his real focus hadn't been on the digital locks. It had been on the emotional ones. He had learned her complex dialect of survival. He learned to never approach her too quickly, especially in the dark. He learned to keep his hands out of his pockets and always tell her when he was entering a room. He watched her hyper-vigilance slowly degrade, month by month, replaced by a cautious, beautiful openness. She was smiling. Her art, while still abstract, was less visceral—less like an underwater scream and more like a vibrant sunrise.

Alex smiled, his heart feeling a profound, unfamiliar warmth as he rolled the bright yellow paint onto the broad expanse of the south wall. Whatever monster had chased her out of the dark fourteen years ago, Alex truly believed he had beaten it. He had built a wall it couldn't scale. He had won the war. A floorboard creaked in the hallway, a soft, familiar sound that Alex's smart system didn't flag, but his internal compass instantly registered. He stopped rolling and turned on the ladder, a natural, grounded grace replacing his calculated movement.

Chloe was standing in the doorway, perfectly framed by the wooden trim and illuminated by the bright morning light flooding the hall. The image of her completely undone, shrinking away from a mirror, was a distant memory. Today, she looked vibrant and anchored. She was wearing low-slung grey leggings and an oversized white button-down shirt—the same one she had stolen from him that first morning, now worn soft and entirely hers. Her dark hair was loosely pulled back in a messy knot, and she was holding a ceramic mug of herbal tea with both hands, breathing in the steam. She looked radiant. She looked safe. And the biggest miracle of all, the variable Alex could never have predicted but now couldn't imagine living without: she was pregnant.

He had just finished tapping off the room when she had walked in, holding a positive test. For the first time in his hyper-rational, risk-averse life, Alex hadn't looked at the logical progression of their timeline. He had just looked at her and known, with absolute, terrifying clarity, that this was the child who would solidify the foundation of the home he was building.

"I was told there would be bright colors," Chloe said, her voice soft and grounded, the trace of trauma entirely absent from her tone. She nodded toward the wall. "The color chart said 'Morning Sunshine.' This looks like you just painted the walls in actual, melted butter."

Alex offered her an effortless smile. "I promised you bright. I just follow the blueprints."

"And is Morning Sunshine proceeding on schedule?" she asked, a faint teasing light in her dark eyes.

Alex looked back at the wall. The yellow was vibrant and warm, completely contrasting with the sterile, grey isolation of her previous life. He thought about the sturdy oak crib that was currently sitting in boxes in the garage. He thought about the small, elegant curves of the ultrasound printout sitting on the nightstand—their little girl. Isabella.

"Ahead of schedule, actually," Alex murmured, his voice dropping into that low, steady register. "Everything is perfectly locked in."

He truly believed it. He had neutralized the ghosts. He had locked the past away forever. He turned back to Chloe, watching her from the ladder. She was smiling, but her left hand had automatically drifted to her lower abdomen, a quiet, unconscious gesture of fierce protection. He saw the shift in her gaze, her eyes darting briefly to the closet door, ensuring it was shut, then to the single window, checking the latch. The hyper-vigilance wasn't gone. It had just been reassigned. She was no longer a soldier on the defensive; she was the protector of the little light growing inside of her.

"Morning Sunshine," she repeated softly, taking a sip of her tea. She walked fully into the room, standing right on the edge of the blue tape line. She reached out and touched the yellow paint, pressing her fingertips against the damp surface. "It feels right."

"We are officially safe in the dark, Chloe," Alex vowed, his analytical mind shutting down, surrendering to the profound, spiritual truth of the moment. "Whatever you ran from is fourteen years too late to catch us now."

He was completely, tragically unaware of the absolute monster he had just challenged to a war he could not win. He thought he was painting a nursery for his daughter. He had no idea he was preparing a shrine for a ghost.

7 THE HEARTBEAT

CHLOE

Clinical spaces are suffocating. Hospitals, clinics, and doctor's offices are built on a foundation of questions, and for the last fourteen years, questions are the most dangerous things in the world. Medical history forms are interrogations.

The bright, sterile fluorescent lights are spotlights designed to expose the jagged, ugly cracks I spend all my energy trying to hide. The thin, sanitary paper crinkles loudly beneath my thighs with every shallow breath. The room smells aggressively of rubbing alcohol, latex gloves, and that distinct, metallic tang of institutional bleach.

My muscles instantly coil tight against the bone. I rest my hands in my lap, my fingers nervously picking at a loose thread on the hem of my oversized sweater. Beneath the thick cotton, my stomach is just beginning to round—a small, undeniable physical curve proving the last twenty weeks aren't a dream.

"You're mapping the exits again." Alex's voice is low, rich, and perfectly steady. It cuts right through the hum of the fluorescent lights.

I glance upward. He sits in a rigid plastic visitor's chair beside the exam table, his long legs stretched out, looking entirely too large for the cramped room. He wears a dark charcoal suit, straight from his corporate office in the financial district.

No stress. No impatience. Just that familiar, unwavering focus. "I'm not," I lie automatically, even though my eyes just finished tracing the path from the solid wooden door to the nearest stairwell sign out in the hallway.

Alex smiles. No argument. He reaches out, covering my trembling, icy hands with his large, warm palm. His thumb traces slow, grounding circles against my knuckles.

"There's only one door," he murmurs softly, leaning in closer so his voice doesn't carry into the hall. "I'm sitting right next to it. Nothing comes in without going through me first. You're safe, Chloe."

I let out a long, shaky exhale, draining the tension from my shoulders. The smell of the bleach fades, replaced by the faint, comforting scent of cedar radiating from his suit jacket. He is the anchor.

He always knows exactly what to say to pull me back from the edge. Before I can form a response, the solid wooden door clicks open. A cheerful ultrasound technician in blue scrubs walks in, holding a thick manila folder.

"Chloe! Alex! So sorry for the wait," she says brightly, glancing at the chart. "Twenty weeks today. The big anatomy scan. Are we ready to take a look at this little one?"

"We are," Alex answers, his grip tightening just a fraction in reassurance. The technician dims the overhead lights, plunging the room into a cool, muted grey.

The sudden darkness sends a sharp, icy spike into my veins, but Alex instantly shifts his chair an inch closer. His knee brushes against my leg. *I'm right here*, the contact says.

I lie back against the crinkling paper, pulling my sweater up to expose my stomach. The technician squirts a generous amount of clear gel onto my skin. The shocking cold forces a sharp gasp.

"Sorry, it's always freezing," she apologizes with a warm laugh, picking up the plastic transducer wand. "Alright, let's see what we have."

She presses the wand firmly against the skin and begins to move it in slow, sweeping arcs. To the right, a large flat screen monitor mounted on the wall instantly flares to life. A chaotic storm of black, grey, and white static.

It looks like one of my manic charcoal sketches before the shadows are forced into a shape. Then, the static parts. A curve of a spine appears.

The perfectly round shape of a skull. A tiny, translucent fist resting near a jawline. "There she is," the technician whispers, her voice softening with genuine awe.

Beside me, Alex stops breathing. His entire body goes completely still. He leans forward, his dark eyes locked onto the glowing monitor, completely captivated by the flickering, grainy image.

The technician presses a button on the console. Suddenly, the quiet room fills with sound. Not a beep or a mechanical hum.

A rapid, rhythmic, thunderous *whoosh-whoosh-whoosh-whoosh*. A train rushing through a tunnel. A wild horse galloping at full speed. Incredibly loud, and undeniably, miraculously alive.

"One hundred and fifty-five beats per minute," the tech announces over the rhythmic thumping. "Strong and perfect."

Alex lets out a breath that sounds like a laugh caught in his throat. He brings my hand up to his lips, pressing a kiss against the knuckles. He looks over, his eyes shining with a moisture that has never been there before.

Back to the monitor. The tiny flutter of the heart valves works on the screen. I'm going to be a mother.

The second the thought fully materializes, a violent, icy spike drives itself straight through the chest. The rhythmic *whoosh-whoosh-whoosh* of the heartbeat suddenly warps. The sound slows down, deepening, shifting pitch until it no longer sounds like a heartbeat.

Thudding, calloused boots walking across a damp floor. *Thud... Thud... Thud...* The sterile walls of the clinic vanish. The kitchenette materializes.

The smell of scorched grease coats the tongue. The yellowed, stained linoleum. The velvet box under the mattress. The tiny, faded "T" embroidered on the ankle of a sock left behind in the dark.

How dare you? A jagged voice whispers in the back of the mind. *How dare you sit in the light and play mother to this child, when you left the first one behind in the cage? You are a fraud. You are a coward.* The chest seizes. Air traps itself in the lungs. My hand goes rigid inside of Alex's grip, an instinctual pull away, the body desperate to curl into a defensive ball. Run.

"Chloe." The voice is sharp, cutting right through the hallucination. Alex doesn't look at the technician.

He doesn't ask what is wrong, and he doesn't draw attention to the sudden, erratic breathing. Instead, he stands up. He moves between me and the door, blocking the peripheral vision of the dark room.

He leans over the exam table, putting his face inches away, forcing eye contact. He smells like cedar and clean soap, entirely banishing the phantom stench of the kitchenette.

"Look at me," he commands softly, his voice a firm, unbreakable anchor.

Wide, terrified eyes meet his. A tear spills hot down the temple into the hairline. "You are right here," Alex whispers fiercely, his dark eyes burning with absolute certainty.

"Whatever ghosts are trying to drag you backward right now, they are not allowed in this room. They don't get to have this. This is ours." He reaches up, his thumb gently catching the tear before it reaches the ear.

"Look at the screen, Chloe," he urges gently. "Look at our daughter. She is safe. And so are you."

I swallow hard, forcing the dense, metallic taste of panic down. I pull a jagged breath of his scent into my lungs. Slowly, agonizingly, I turn my head back toward the glowing monitor.

The tiny fist is still there. The rapid, beautiful *whoosh-whoosh-whoosh* fills the air, drowning out the phantom footsteps. Looking at the flickering shape of Isabella, I make a conscious, terrifying choice to fight the dark.

I choose to stay. I choose to let the joy win. A sob breaks free, loud and ungraceful. Not a sound of terror.

I squeeze Alex's hand with all the strength left in my bones, tears of pure, unadulterated relief spilling over my cheeks. I am staying in the light.

8 THE ANCHOR

ALEX

There was a profound, grounding satisfaction in building something with your own two hands. Alex knelt on the plush, cream-colored rug in the center of the yellow nursery, a small steel Allen wrench gripped firmly between his fingers. He gave the thick, recessed bolt one final, aggressive twist, sinking it flush into the solid oak frame. The metal groaned in protest before locking perfectly into place.

He dropped the wrench onto the carpet and wiped a bead of sweat from his brow with the back of his wrist. He placed his hands on the top rail of the crib and gave it a violent shake, testing the structural integrity. It didn't budge a single millimeter. It was a fortress.

Alex sat back on his heels, letting out a long, deep exhale as he surveyed the room. The late afternoon sun poured through the wide window, catching the golden hues of the "Morning Sunshine" paint and casting long, warm shadows across the floorboards. The room smelled of fresh linen, new wood, and the faint, sweet scent of the baby powder Chloe had meticulously organized on the changing table just that morning. He leaned against the base of the crib, stretching his legs out in front of him.

If someone had told him a year ago that his greatest professional achievement wouldn't be launching a multi-million dollar financial software platform, but successfully assembling a piece of baby furniture without missing a single wooden dowel, he would have laughed. But looking around this room, the corporate world felt entirely insignificant. He thought about the timeline. The sheer velocity of their healing over the last several months was nothing short of a miracle.

In the beginning, loving Chloe had been an exercise in emotional bomb disposal. He remembered the nights she would wake up thrashing, eyes wide and unseeing, scrambling backward against the headboard to escape the shadows. He remembered the way she used to map out the exits of every restaurant, the way she would physically flinch if a door closed too loudly, and the obsessive, rhythmic clicking of the apartment deadbolts—three times, every single night. But over the last six months, as the pregnancy progressed, that terrified girl had slowly, beautifully faded away.

She didn't check the locks anymore. He hadn't seen her flinch at a loud noise since the day at the ultrasound clinic. Her art had transformed, shifting from those violent, bleeding slashes of cadmium red to sweeping, ethereal landscapes painted in soft blues and bright golds. Alex rested his hand against the smooth oak spindle of the crib. He felt an overwhelming, swelling tide of pride in his chest.

He had done it. He had provided the exact environment she needed to heal. He didn't know the specifics of the nightmare she had run from all those years ago, and he had made peace with the fact that he probably never would. He didn't need the data. He didn't need the names or the locations. All that mattered was that the dark was gone, replaced entirely by the bright, unshaded walls of this yellow room.

"You look like a man who just conquered a mountain."

Alex turned his head. Chloe was standing in the doorway, barefoot and glowing. She was wearing a soft, oversized grey knit sweater that stretched comfortably over the pronounced, beautiful swell of her seven-month pregnancy. Her dark hair fell in loose, effortless waves over her shoulders, and there was a faint, dusty smudge of violet paint on the tip of her nose. She didn't look like a survivor bracing for an impact. She looked like a mother.

"I conquered the Swedish instruction manual," Alex corrected with a soft smile, gesturing to the crumpled paper booklet tossed in the corner of the room. "Which, frankly, requires more strategic planning than a mountain."

Chloe laughed, the sound bright and entirely unburdened. She walked fully into the room, her hand resting instinctively on her stomach. She didn't hesitate or scan the corners. She walked straight to him, lowering herself carefully onto the plush rug until she was sitting cross-legged right beside him. She leaned her head against his shoulder. He immediately wrapped his arm around her, pulling her warm weight flush against his side. He pressed a kiss into her hair, breathing in the scent of her lavender shampoo and the lingering smell of oil paint.

"It's perfect," she whispered, her eyes tracing the solid lines of the oak crib, the carefully folded pastel blankets, and the small, plush elephant sitting on the dresser. "It's exactly what I pictured. It’s so quiet."

"Quiet is good," Alex murmured, his hand dropping to rest over hers on her stomach. "Quiet is the baseline now."

"I was thinking about Dr. Aris," Chloe said, her voice light and conversational, referring to the pediatrician they had interviewed the week prior. "She mentioned that the elementary school down the street has that incredible art immersion program. I know it's five years away, but..."

"But we need to get on the waitlist," Alex finished for her, smiling at the mundane, beautiful normality of the conversation.

"Exactly," Chloe nodded, turning her face to look up at him, her dark eyes shining with an emotion he had never seen there before—pure, unadulterated hope. "I want her to have all of it, Alex. Field trips. Finger painting. Piano lessons that she hates but we make her go to anyway. I want her to have the most boring, wonderfully normal childhood in the history of the world."

Alex felt a tight, emotional lump form in his throat. Hearing her talk about the future—a future stretching five, ten years down the road—was the ultimate proof of his victory. She was no longer living day-to-day, bracing for the floor to drop out beneath her. She was building a foundation.

"She will," Alex vowed, his voice dropping into a solemn, unbreakable promise. "She's going to have everything. And she's never going to know a single day of fear. Not in this house."

Right on cue, as if reacting to the deep rumble of his voice, Isabella kicked. It was a sharp, distinct flutter against Alex's palm. He gasped slightly, his eyes widening in pure wonder as he looked down at Chloe's stomach.

"Did you feel that?" Chloe asked, a breathless laugh escaping her lips as she covered his hand with both of hers, holding it firmly against the kick.

"I felt it," Alex breathed out, completely awestruck. He shifted his body, leaning down until his forehead was resting gently against the soft curve of her stomach. "I feel you, Isabella. I've got you."

Chloe ran her fingers softly through his dark hair, the movement slow, rhythmic, and incredibly soothing. They sat there in the fading sunlight, anchored to the floorboards of their perfect, impenetrable fortress. Alex closed his eyes, letting the warmth of his wife and the physical proof of his daughter wash away the last lingering shadows of his anxiety.

He was an architect who had finally finished his masterpiece. The walls were fortified. The perimeter was secure. He had stared down the terrifying, anonymous ghosts of Chloe's past, and he had starved them out with love, patience, and unyielding stability. There were no secrets left in the dark that could possibly touch them here.

He was absolutely certain of it.

9 THE BURIAL

CHLOE

For the first time in my life, the canvas is entirely quiet. The late morning sunlight pours through the sheer white curtains of the spare room, pooling warmly on the hardwood floor. I hold a wide, flat bristle brush loosely in my right hand.

Not gripped like a weapon. No violent scraping of charcoal across paper at three in the morning. I glide the bristles across the canvas in smooth, unbroken, sweeping arcs.

No cadmium red. No bruised purples or suffocating, ash-grey shadows. The palette is filled with cerulean blue, soft titanium white, and a pale, shimmering gold.

A sky. Not a suffocating, oppressive city sky trapping the air beneath it, but an immense, open expanse of dawn. A painting specifically meant to hang above Isabella's oak crib.

I take a step back. I tilt my head, studying the soft gradient of light spreading across the fabric. I pull a deep, steady breath into my lungs.

The air in the house smells of lemon oil and the faint, sweet trace of herbal tea. I close my eyes, waiting for the familiar, phantom scent of damp wood and scorched grease to creep up from behind. Waiting for the crushing weight of trauma to serve its reminder that I don't deserve to paint the dawn.

The smell never comes. The weight doesn't drop. The heart beats in a steady, calm, perfectly normal rhythm against the ribs.

Right at that exact moment, as if confirming the absolute safety of the room, Isabella kicks. Not a gentle flutter this time. A sharp, distinct, powerful jab directly against my lower ribs.

A soft gasp escapes my lips. I drop the paintbrush onto the wooden tray. I move both hands to the swell of my stomach, pressing my palms firmly against the spot where she struck.

"I know," I whisper, a breathless, tearful smile breaking across my face. "I feel you, little one. I'm right here."

She kicks again, rolling beneath my hands. A fierce, territorial, and entirely primitive instinct flares in the chest, burning hotter than any anxiety I have ever known. An instinct forbidden for fourteen years.

I am a mother. Not a sixteen-year-old girl trapped on a linoleum floor, paralyzed by a man sharpening a hunting knife. Not a ghost haunting my own life.

A grown woman standing in a house fortified by love, carrying a daughter who will never, ever know the meaning of the dark. I look back at the canvas, the golden light of the painted sunrise glowing.

The shadows cannot come into this new world. Isabella cannot inherit these ghosts. To truly be her mother—the fierce, unyielding shield Alex believes me to be—the child I couldn't save has to be let go.

I turn away from the easel and walk out of the studio. My bare feet make no sound against the hardwood as I move down the wide hallway toward the master bedroom. No hesitation.

No mapping the exits. I walk straight to the side of the broad king-sized bed, dropping to my knees on the plush rug. I reach my arm deep into the narrow, dark gap between the mattress and the box spring.

My fingers blindly brush against the soft fabric of the fitted sheet before finally grazing the cold, hard brass latch of the small wooden box. I pull it out into the light.

Weighted, as if fourteen years of suffocating guilt and silence, screaming night terrors are condensed into this single, solid object. Inside, resting on the faded dark velvet, is the yellowed infant's sock with the tiny, embroidered "T".

My thumb hovers over the mechanical latch. The dark, familiar voice—the echo of Artie—whispers from the shadows of memory. *Open it, Chloe. Look at what you left behind. Punish yourself. You don't get to be happy.* The pulse flutters in the throat. Breathing grows shallow. The urge to flip the latch, to stare at the cotton sock and drown in the familiar, agonizing current of self-hatred, is a gravitational pull.

An addiction. The survival tactic for fourteen years—keeping the wound actively bleeding so it is never forgotten. Isabella rolls against my ribs again.

The movement is a physical anchor, yanking everything violently back to the present. I look down at my stomach, then back at the wooden box.

"No." My voice is raspy, but absolutely firm. The word hangs in the air, severing the invisible thread connecting this room to the kitchenette.

"You don't get to come with me," I whisper, a single, hot tear spilling over my lower lash line. "I'm sorry. I am so, so sorry. But I can't carry you anymore."

The latch stays closed. I push off the floor, holding the box tightly against my chest. I walk across the bedroom to the expansive walk-in closet.

I flick the overhead light on, illuminating rows of Alex's impeccably pressed suits and soft, oversized sweaters. Sitting on the floor in the corner of the closet is a large, opaque plastic storage bin filled with old winter scarves and thick, knitted blankets.

I kneel down and pop the plastic lid off the bin. My hands dig deep into the thick wool fabric, creating a dark, insulated cavity at the very bottom. My trembling hands lower the small wooden box into the center of the blankets.

No lingering. No prayers. I fold the thick wool over the top, burying the box completely out of sight. I snap the plastic lid back onto the bin, the sound loud and definitive in the quiet closet.

But that isn't enough. It can't just be hidden; it has to be unreachable. I drag a small wooden step stool over from Alex's side of the closet.

I lift the large plastic bin, my muscles straining slightly under the awkward weight. I climb two steps up. I slide the bin onto the very highest shelf, past the empty luggage, shoving it all the way to the absolute back corner, wedging it tightly against the drywall where the light can't reach it.

I step down and dust off my hands. I stare up at the dark corner. I wait for the guilt to crush me.

I wait for the panic attack to hit, for the lungs to seize up in protest of the betrayal. Instead, a profound, overwhelming wave of physical exhaustion washes over, immediately followed by an incredible, buoyant sense of lightness.

The crushing lead apron worn over the ribs for an entire adult life is gone. The ghost is buried. The past is locked away, shoved into the dark where it can no longer dictate the future.

I wipe the tear away from my cheek. I click the closet light off, leaving the velvet box in the absolute dark. Out in the sunlit bedroom, a deep, clean breath of cedar-scented air fills my lungs.

I am ready to be Isabella's mother. I am ready to live in the light. Completely, beautifully unaware that ghosts do not stay buried forever, and the lock placed on the past is about to violently shatter.

10 THE GLASS HOUSE

CHLOE

The track lighting in the downtown Birmingham gallery is blinding, clinical, and absolutely inescapable. I stand in the center of the polished hardwood floor, wearing a tailored, emerald-green maternity dress that perfectly accentuates the swell of my stomach.

In my left hand, I hold a crystal glass of sparkling cider. My right hand is occupied by a relentless, exhausting parade of handshakes. To the wealthy, perfumed patrons of Metro Detroit, I am the ultimate success story.

I am the enigmatic, brilliant artist who translates raw emotion into breathtaking abstract canvases. I am the glowing, expectant mother. I am the beautiful wife of a highly successful corporate risk manager.

I am a masterpiece of curated fiction. A tall, silver-haired man in a bespoke suit leans in too close, his expensive cologne briefly overwhelming the scent of lilies arranged on the catering tables.

He gestures toward my latest canvas, a stark, jagged collision of cerulean blue and titanium white. "The isolation in this piece is just visceral, Chloe," the man says, swirling his champagne. "It feels so... trapped. Tell me, where do you draw that kind of profound darkness from? A difficult childhood?"

My knuckles bleach white against the stem of my crystal glass. The muscles in my neck tighten. For a fraction of a second, the pristine white walls of the gallery dissolve, replaced by the suffocating smell of damp earth and scorched grease.

"Imagination," I lie smoothly, offering him a practiced, porcelain smile. "Just the human condition, Richard. We all have our shadows."

"Brilliant," he murmurs, entirely satisfied with the illusion. As he steps away, a manicured hand grips my elbow.

It is Nina. She is wearing a flawless charcoal pantsuit, orchestrating the room with the ruthless efficiency of a general. But as she looks at the painting, her grip on my arm is trembling.

"Three pieces sold in the first hour," Nina whispers, though her eyes don't reflect the triumph of a gallery owner. They look hollow. "They love the pain, Chloe. They pay a premium for the dark because they don't have to actually live in it."

I look at Nina. I see the quiet, desperate guilt she has carried for five thousand days. Every canvas she sells for me is a down payment on a debt she knows we can never actually clear.

"I need a minute, Nina," I whisper, the suffocating heat of the crowded room pressing against my throat. "It's too loud."

"Of course," Nina says, her composure instantly returning. "Go. Breathe. You've earned it."

I turn away from the glaring track lights, desperate for a quiet corner, but the crowd is a dense, impenetrable wall of silk and tailored wool. I close my eyes, a sudden, terrifying wave of vertigo washing over me. The phantom walls of the cage begin to close in.

Then, the sea of patrons suddenly parts.

ALEX

Alex moved through the crowded gallery with the imposing, undeniable presence of an icebreaker carving through a frozen sea. He wasn't looking at the art. He had spent the last two hours tracking the precise micro-expressions on his wife's face. He knew the exact difference between her polite, social smile and the rigid, breathless mask she wore when the trauma was threatening to pull her under. When her hand drifted defensively over her pregnant stomach and her eyes darted toward the exit, Alex intervened. He reached Chloe, placing his broad, warm hand firmly against the small of her back. It was the physical anchor she relied on.

"We're done," Alex murmured, his mouth close to her ear. "I'm taking you home." He didn't wait for her to argue. Alex guided her through the final cluster of patrons, shielding her fragile frame with his own rugged shoulders. He pushed the solid glass doors of the gallery open, and the freezing, sharp winter air of Michigan hit them like a physical wave. The snow had already started to fall, thick and blinding.

An hour later, they were miles away from the noise, the critics, and the suffocating pressure of the public eye. Alex stood in the threshold of the spare bedroom, his shoulder leaning heavily against the pristine white doorframe. His hands were tucked casually into the pockets of his dark denim jeans. He had spent his entire adult life waiting for the other shoe to drop, but as he looked into the room before him, his anxious mind came up completely empty. The nursery was completely, undeniably finished. The walls, painted in that vibrant, unapologetic "Morning Sunshine" yellow, seemed to generate their own internal heat, glowing softly under the dim, warm setting of the track lighting. In the center of the room stood the sturdy, solid oak crib he had built with his own hands. Draped perfectly over the thick wooden rail was a hand-knitted pastel blanket. He let his eyes drift to the open closet. Hanging from the wooden rod, perfectly spaced and categorized by month, were dozens of impossibly small, soft cotton outfits.

Alex let out a slow, steady breath. The air in the room smelled like clean linen, baby powder, and the faint, sweet trace of lavender. He shifted his gaze toward the large, double-paned window at the far end of the room. Outside, Detroit was being buried under the first blinding snowstorm of the winter season. The wind was howling, a low, vicious sound that rattled the bare branches of the oak trees in their front yard. But inside the house Alex had built, the elements couldn't reach them. The air hummed at a perfect, steady seventy-two degrees. The perimeter was secured by reinforced deadbolts and a top-tier security system.

Sitting in the plush, oversized cream rocking chair in the corner of the nursery was Chloe. She wore a pair of soft grey sweatpants and one of Alex’s oversized cashmere sweaters. Her dark hair was falling in loose, effortless waves. She was holding a small, plush elephant in her hands, her thumbs absentmindedly tracing the soft fabric of its ears as she watched the violent snowstorm rage against the glass. She wasn't mapping the exits. She wasn't faking a smile for a gallery patron. She was completely, beautifully at rest.

Alex pushed off the doorframe and walked quietly into the room. His footsteps were muffled by the thick rug. Chloe didn't flinch. She simply turned her head, a soft, sleepy smile breaking across her face. Her dark eyes, which had once looked like shattered glass, were clear and warm.

"It's really coming down out there," she murmured, her voice a low, peaceful hum.

"Lake effect," Alex replied softly, stepping up behind the rocking chair. He rested his hands gently on her shoulders. "The news said we might get eight inches by morning."

"Good," Chloe whispered, leaning her head back against his stomach. "Let it snow. We don't have to be anywhere."

Alex shifted his hands, letting his arms slide down over her collarbone until his large hands were resting gently over the pronounced swell of her stomach. Beneath his palms, Isabella shifted—a slow, sleepy roll that sent a profound, electrical jolt of love straight through his chest. "We have everything we need right in this room," Alex agreed, resting his chin on the top of her head. They stayed like that for a long time. The only sounds in the house were the rhythmic, soothing creak of the rocking chair, the low howl of the winter wind outside, and the steady, synchronized cadence of their breathing.

"Alex?" Chloe's voice broke the quiet, carrying a weight of sudden, immense vulnerability.

"I'm right here," he answered, his grip tightening instinctively.

She stopped rocking the chair. She reached up, placing her hands firmly over his where they rested on her stomach. "I used to think that the dark was a permanent condition," she said, her words deliberate and measured. "When you sat down at my table in that coffee shop... I was so incredibly broken. I was just waiting for the world to finally finish crushing me."

Alex swallowed hard, his throat tightening. "You weren't broken, Chloe. You were surviving."

"I was a ghost," she corrected gently, opening her eyes to look at the yellow walls. "But you didn't run. You just... stood between me and the noise. You built this." She gestured with a slight nod toward the crib, the pastel clothes, the entire fortress around them. "You saved my life."

"You did the hard work," Alex countered, his voice rough with emotion. He leaned down, pressing a long, reverent kiss to her temple. "I just gave you a safe place to stand."

Chloe turned her face, pressing a kiss against the inside of his wrist. "I buried it, Alex," she whispered, her voice cracking slightly, tears pooling in her dark eyes. "The fear. The past. Whatever it was that kept me locked in the dark... I let it go. I'm finally free."

Alex felt an immense, invisible weight lift off his own shoulders. It was the final verbal confirmation of his victory. The war was officially over.

"I know," Alex said, his voice a low, unbreakable vow. "I've got you. And I've got her. No one is ever going to hurt you again."

An hour later, they left the golden warmth of the nursery. Alex shut the solid white door with a soft, definitive click. He walked down the dark hallway to the master bedroom. He checked the digital security panel on the wall. The glowing green light confirmed that all exterior doors were locked, all windows were sealed, and the perimeter was completely secure. He climbed into the broad king-sized bed, pulling the thick duvet up over them. Chloe immediately shifted her weight, curling her back flush against his chest, her breathing evening out almost instantly as she surrendered to a deep, dreamless sleep.

Alex lay awake for a few minutes longer, staring up at the dark ceiling. Outside, the snow continued to bury the city, freezing the world into a state of absolute, unmoving silence. Inside, the house was perfectly still. The doors were locked. The nursery was waiting. His wife and his daughter were safe in his arms. Alex closed his eyes, resting in the absolute, undeniable certainty that his life was permanently secure. He fell asleep feeling utterly untouchable.

11 **THE CATALYST**

CHLOE

The snow stops falling sometime before dawn, leaving the world completely paralyzed beneath two feet of thick, blinding white. I lay perfectly still on my back, staring up at the bedroom ceiling. The house is completely silent.

But it isn't the warm, peaceful quiet of the night before. This silence is absolute. It is a suffocating, unnatural stillness that makes the air in the room feel too thin to breathe.

I press my hands over the pronounced swell of my stomach, waiting for the familiar, energetic flutter of Isabella waking up. I wait for the sharp little kick against the lower ribs. Nothing.

A full minute passes. The silence stretches out, shifting from peaceful to something distinctly terrifying.

"Come on, little one," I whisper, my thumbs gently rubbing the sides of my stomach. The pulse begins to thrum in my throat. "Time to wake up."

Still nothing. Just a profound, hollow stillness resting beneath my palms. A microscopic needle of unease pricks the back of the neck.

I immediately push it away, deploying the logic Alex built. Babies sleep. It's normal. She's just resting.

I take a deep, jagged breath, forcing the hyper-vigilance down. I push the thick duvet aside. I swing my legs over the edge of the mattress.

As soon as my bare feet touch the hardwood floor, a sudden, violent cramp seizes the lower abdomen. Not a flutter. Not a kick.

A sharp, tearing sensation, like a jagged piece of glass dragged across the insides. I gasp. Hands instinctively fly to the stomach, and I double over, resting my forehead against my knees.

The pain flares hot and brilliant, then slowly recedes into a dull, throbbing ache. Braxton Hicks. My frantic rationalization tries to keep up with a dangerously accelerating heart rate.

Dr. Aris said they can start around this time. It's normal. Everything is normal.

My shaky legs force themselves to stand, completely drained of strength. I take a step toward the en-suite bathroom. With every movement, the dragging, hollow sensation in the stomach pulls downward—a terrifying gravitational pull that catches the breath in the throat.

I push the bathroom door open. The bright vanity lights automatically flicker on. I take a few steps to the toilet.

As I pull my soft grey sweatpants down, a flash of color strikes my eyes. Not the soft, muted pastels of the nursery. Not the warm, glowing yellow of Morning Sunshine. Red.

Vibrant, violent, unmistakable cadmium red. Staining the fabric of the clothes. Pooling on the pristine white porcelain. Everywhere.

Time completely stops. The ambient noise of the house vanishes entirely, sucked into a terrifying vacuum. My mind refuses to process the data.

It is an impossible variable. It breaks every single rule of the fortress Alex built. I am safe.

The box is buried. The past is gone. This isn't supposed to happen. Then, the second cramp hits.

Infinitely worse than the first. A brutal, agonizing contraction that drops me instantly to my knees. Bare skin hits the freezing marble tiles with a sickening thud.

I wrap my arms around my stomach, curling into a tight, desperate ball. A ragged, breathless sound tears its way out of the throat. No. No. Please, no.

I squeeze my eyes shut, praying to a god ignored for fourteen years. Please. I'll take the nightmares back. I'll take the panic attacks.

Just don't take her. Please don't take her. But the pain doesn't stop. It radiates through the lower back, a rhythmic, agonizing pulse signaling the end of the world.

As the physical pain peaks, the psychological dam violently shatters. The pristine smell of the marble bathroom is instantly obliterated by the phantom stench of damp wood, cheap alcohol, and scorched grease.

The sterile white vanity lights flicker, warping into the sickly, jaundiced yellow of a dying overhead bulb. The smooth, heated marble beneath the knees transforms into cracked, sticky linoleum. The border between reality and the nightmare completely dissolves.

The silence of the house is broken by the sound of thudding, calloused boots walking across the floorboards. *Thud... Thud... Thud...* The air in the bathroom grows suffocatingly tight.

Lungs seize in absolute terror. The ghost from the top shelf of the closet is standing right behind the glass shower door.

Did you really think you could escape? The voice isn't an auditory hallucination. It is physically present, a dry, raspy whisper scraping directly against the inside of the ear. Artie.

Did you really think you were allowed to just start over? He hisses, smelling of ash and malice. *Did you think you could just replace her? You left Tyra in the dark. And now, the dark is taking this one, too.* "No!" My scream is raw and jagged, echoing violently against the tile. "No, leave her alone! She's mine!"

Bloody hands slip on the marble as I frantically scramble backward, pressing into the corner between the glass shower and the wall. This isn't a medical emergency anymore. It is cosmic, inescapable retribution.

The universe isn't just taking my baby; it is punishing a coward. *Rule number one*, the ghost whispers, a cruel, mocking echo vibrating through the teeth. *Tyra.* "Chloe?!" The bathroom door bursts open, slamming violently against the drywall. Alex stands in the threshold.

He looks at me in the corner. Then, his eyes track down to the bright red blood smeared across the white marble floor. The dish towel drops from his hand. His warm, dark complexion instantly turns ashen.

"Alex!" I reach a trembling, bloodstained hand out toward him. "Alex, please! He's taking her! He's taking her!"

He drops to his knees, sliding across the tile. He pulls me violently into his chest, wrapping strong arms around my shoulders, trying to physically shield me from a force he can't see.

"I've got you," he chokes out. Hands shake frantically as he pulls his phone from his pocket, dialing 911. "I'm right here. Hold on, Chloe. Please, just hold on."

But the grip slips. Another brutal contraction rips through the body. The last ounce of hope drains out, leaving nothing but an empty, echoing void.

I go completely limp in Alex's arms, letting the screaming sirens in the distance fade into static. I close my eyes and surrender to the dark, knowing with absolute certainty that this is exactly where I belong.

12 THE FALLOUT

ALEX

There are certain moments in life that permanently divide your timeline into a before and an after. Alex sat in a rigid plastic chair in the surgical waiting room of the hospital, staring down at his hands. They were stained. The stark, harsh fluorescent lights above buzzed with a low, mechanical hum, casting a sickly, sterile glare over the room. He was still wearing his grey T-shirt and the canvas kitchen apron, both ruined by wide, dark swaths of cadmium red. He hadn't washed his hands. He hadn't changed. He hadn't moved a single muscle in two hours. To wash the blood away felt like a betrayal. It felt like erasing the last physical evidence that Isabella had ever existed.

A set of solid double doors swung open at the end of the corridor. The sound echoed like a gunshot in the empty waiting area. Alex lifted his head slowly, his neck stiff, his eyes burning with a dry, exhausted heat. A doctor in pale green scrubs was walking toward him. Her expression was neutral, professional, and completely devastating. She didn't have the hurried, frantic energy of someone rushing to save a life. She had the slow, measured pace of someone carrying a profound, immovable truth. Alex stood up. His imposing frame felt hollow, as if his bones had been replaced by ash.

"Alex," the doctor said softly as she stopped in front of him, folding her hands in front of her. She didn't need to say anything else. Alex read the data in the slight dip of her shoulders and the profound, clinical pity in her eyes. The fortress he had spent the last year meticulously building, reinforcing, and defending had just been leveled to the ground by an invisible earthquake.

"I'm so sorry," she continued, her voice gentle but firm. "It was a severe placental abruption. It happened incredibly fast. There was absolutely nothing we could do to stop it. We lost the baby."

The words didn't register as sound; they registered as physical blows to his sternum. "Chloe?" Alex managed to ask, his voice a jagged, unrecognizable rasp.

"She is physically stable," the doctor assured him quickly. "We had to perform an emergency D&C to stop the hemorrhaging, but she is recovering. She's in room 412. You can go back and see her now. But Alex..." The doctor hesitated, her brow furrowing slightly. "She is in a state of profound shock. She hasn't spoken a word since we brought her out of the operating room."

Alex nodded blindly. He bypassed the doctor, pushing his way through the double doors and stepping into the sterile labyrinth of the surgical recovery wing. Room 412 was dark. The only illumination came from the rhythmic, glowing green line of the heart monitor next to the bed and the pale, grey winter light filtering through the frosted window blinds. Alex stepped into the room. The air smelled of iodine and strong sedatives.

Chloe was sitting up slightly in the hospital bed, propped against a thin, starched pillow. She was wearing a faded, generic hospital gown. But it wasn't the clothes that made Alex's heart seize; it was her eyes. The vibrant, radiant woman who had smiled at him in the yellow nursery just twelve hours ago was entirely gone. The dark, haunted, terrified ghost from the Midtown coffee shop had returned, and she had taken total possession of his wife. Chloe was staring blankly at the blank television screen mounted on the opposite wall. Her rich complexion had faded to a sickly ash, her lips dry and cracked. She wasn't crying. She wasn't trembling. She was perfectly, terrifyingly still. She had completely retreated behind the impenetrable, jagged walls of her trauma.

"Chloe," Alex whispered, his voice breaking as he stepped up to the edge of the bed. She didn't blink. She didn't acknowledge the sound of his voice. Desperate to anchor her, desperate to prove that he was still here to protect her, Alex reached out. He slowly lowered his large, warm hand, intending to cover her small, trembling fingers resting on the white blanket.

The second his skin brushed hers, she reacted. It wasn't a gentle withdrawal. It was a violent, instinctual flinch. Her entire body recoiled, her hand snatching away from his touch as if she had been burned. She shrank back against the pillows, her breath hitching in her throat, her dark eyes finally darting to his face. But she wasn't looking at him with love. She was looking at him with absolute, unadulterated terror.

Alex froze, his hand suspended in the empty air above the bed. The physical rejection tore through him, infinitely more painful than the devastating news the doctor had just delivered. She didn't want him. She didn't trust him. The safety he had promised her had failed, and now, she was actively punishing herself, believing she was entirely contaminated by the dark. He slowly lowered his hand to his side, stepping back to give her the space she was silently screaming for.

"Okay," he whispered, a single tear finally breaking free and tracking hot down his face. "I'm right here. I won't touch you. I'm just going to sit right here." He pulled a plastic chair to the corner of the room, sitting down in the shadows. He stayed there for six hours, watching the woman he loved drown in a silent ocean he had no idea how to navigate.

They drove home in absolute silence. The violent snowstorm had finally passed, leaving the Detroit suburbs buried under a thick, suffocating blanket of white. The streets were empty.

The sky was a bruised, heavy grey. Alex pulled the large SUV into their driveway. The house loomed in front of them, the security lights casting long, sharp shadows across the unbroken snow. Just yesterday, this house had been the ultimate symbol of his victory. It had been their sanctuary. Now, as Alex unlocked the front door and pushed it open, the warm air of the heater rushing out to greet them, it felt like stepping into a tomb.

The silence inside was deafening. Every pristine, secure detail of the house now felt like a cruel, twisted joke. The digital keypad on the wall. The perfectly aligned shoes in the entryway. The faint, lingering smell of the espresso he had made that morning. It was a perfectly maintained graveyard.

Chloe stepped over the threshold. She moved like a sleepwalker, her movements stiff, completely devoid of the natural, grounded grace she had fought so hard to find. She didn't take off her coat. She didn't look at Alex. Without saying a single word, she began to walk slowly down the dark hallway. Alex stood frozen in the entryway, watching her go.

As she passed the spare bedroom, Alex held his breath. The white door was cracked open just an inch, casting a thin, dark sliver of a shadow across the hardwood floor. Inside that room were the vibrant yellow walls. Inside that room was the heavy oak crib. Chloe didn't even turn her head. She walked past the yellow room as if it didn't exist, her eyes locked dead ahead. She reached the end of the hallway and stepped into the master bedroom. She pulled the door shut behind her.

Alex stood alone in the quiet house, the weight of his absolute failure pressing down on his shoulders. He waited, his chest tight, listening to the suffocating silence. Then, he heard it. *Click*. It was a sharp, metallic sound. It was the sound of the solid deadbolt sliding firmly into place from the inside of the bedroom door.

Alex closed his eyes, dropping his chin to his chest as a fresh wave of quiet, agonizing grief washed over him. He had spent the last year meticulously checking the perimeter. He had built the strongest walls he could imagine to keep the monsters out. But as he stood alone in the dark hallway, listening to the echoes of the locked door, he finally realized the terrifying truth. The walls hadn't failed. The monster had been inside the house the entire time…

TYRA

The dark was not empty. The dark had a texture, a weight, and a sound. Fourteen-year-old Tyra sat in the deepest corner of the concrete cell, her knees pulled tightly to her chest, her thin arms wrapped around her shins. She was perfectly still. She had learned a long time ago that movement generated noise, and noise drew the dark closer. The air in the room was freezing, smelling permanently of damp earth, rusted metal, and the sharp, metallic tang of her own unwashed skin. Above her, the ceiling was a solid slab of reinforced steel. There were no windows. There was no concept of day or night, only the agonizing stretches of silence broken by the heavy, thudding footsteps on the dirt floor above.

She waited, her breath shallow. *Thud. Thud. Thud.* The footsteps were moving down the wooden stairs. Tyra squeezed her eyes shut, pressing her back so hard against the freezing concrete she felt the jagged ridges biting through her thin, frayed sweater. At the end of the short hallway, the heavy steel door groaned. Then came the sound that defined her entire existence: the sharp, definitive clack of a heavy iron padlock snapping open.

A blinding wedge of artificial yellow light pierced the pitch-black room. Tyra flinched, throwing a dirty, trembling hand over her eyes. A towering silhouette filled the doorway. Arthur Vance stepped into the cell. He was a mountain of a man, clad in a heavy thermal coat and rugged, snow-caked boots. His thick beard was wild, his eyes hidden beneath the shadow of a dark woolen cap. He didn't look like a monster; he looked like a pioneer who had survived the end of the world. He was holding an aluminum tray.

"Tyra," his voice rumbled, low and startlingly gentle. It echoed off the concrete walls.

Tyra slowly lowered her hand, her dark, hollow eyes tracking his movements with feral intensity. She didn't speak. Her throat, completely unused to casual conversation, felt like it was lined with sandpaper. Artie knelt on the freezing floor, placing the tray down. A bowl of steaming, unseasoned oatmeal and a plastic cup of water. He didn't push it toward her. He waited patiently for her to realize it was safe.

"It's freezing up there tonight," Artie said, pulling off one of his heavy leather gloves. He reached out, his massive, calloused hand gently brushing a matted strand of dark hair out of Tyra's eyes. She trembled violently under his touch, but she didn't pull away. To pull away was ungrateful. "The snow is burying the trees," he continued softly. "The world out there is freezing over. It's a sick, dying place, Tyra. Full of poison. Full of people who want to hurt you, infect you, and take away your purity."

He gestured to the solid concrete walls around them. "But the rot can't get through the steel," Artie whispered, his eyes shining with a dark, absolute conviction. "I built this place to keep the sickness out. I built this place to keep you safe."

Tyra looked at the bowl of oatmeal. Her stomach clawed at her ribs, a violent, hollow ache. She slowly reached out a trembling, dirt-streaked hand and pulled the tray closer. Artie watched her eat for a long moment, a twisted look of paternal pride settling over his hardened features.

"Do you remember the story, Tyra?" he asked quietly. "Do you remember the girl who left?"

Tyra froze, the plastic spoon halfway to her mouth. She gave a small, jerky nod.

"She was weak," Artie said, his voice dropping into a cold, venomous register. "She didn't want to be safe. She wanted the poison. She climbed out the window and let the sickness of the world take her. She abandoned you to the wolves because she was a liar and a coward."

Artie stood up, his massive frame blotting out the light from the hallway. "She is a ghost, Tyra. And ghosts only want to drag you into the cold." He reached down and picked up the heavy iron padlock. "But I will never leave you. As long as I lock this door, the poison can never reach you."

"Thank you," Tyra rasped. It was a broken, conditioned whisper. The ultimate surrender of a mind that had been molded in the dark. "Thank you, Dad."

Artie smiled. It was a terrifying, genuine expression of love. He stepped backward out of the cell. The heavy steel door slammed shut, plunging Tyra instantly back into the absolute, suffocating pitch-black. A second later, the iron padlock clicked into place, sealing her inside the earth. Tyra sat alone in the dark, eating her cold oatmeal, utterly terrified of the phantom mother who had left her behind, and entirely grateful to the monster who kept the door locked.

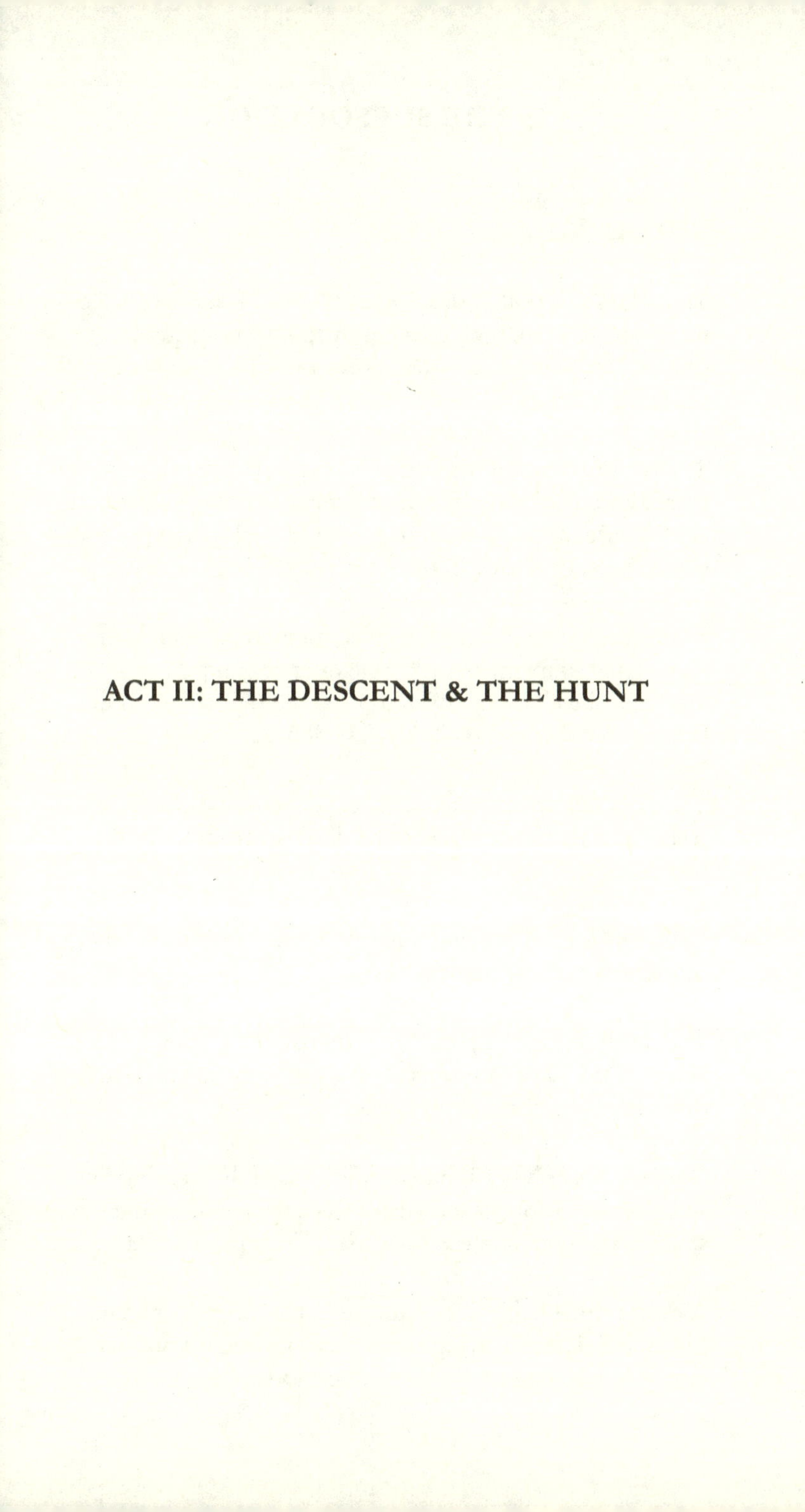

ACT II: THE DESCENT & THE HUNT

13 **THE SUFFOCATION**

CHLOE

Time does not heal; it simply gathers dust. Four days since the hospital. I pull my knees tightly to my chest, swallowed by one of Alex's oversized wool sweaters in the exact center of the living room sofa.

The physical pain of the surgery is a dull, constant throb. But there is no medication for the crushing, echoing void where Isabella used to be. Across the room, the television plays a muted cooking show.

From the kitchen, I hear the quiet, methodical sounds of Alex trying to maintain order. He operates on pure, mechanical willpower, trying to keep the framework of our lives from collapsing. But the glass house is already shattered.

The doorbell rings. A sharp, cheerful, two-tone chime. It feels violently out of place in the dead, stagnant air of the room.

I don't move. I don't even turn my head. Alex's thudding footsteps cross the hardwood floor.

The deadbolts click open. The solid oak door swings wide. "Mom. Dad," Alex's voice is low, thick with an exhaustion that makes the chest physically ache.

"Oh, my sweet boy," Linda answers, instantly breaking into a soft, shattered sob. The rustle of thick winter coats and the shuffling of boots on the floor mat. Alex's parents are here.

A cold, primal panic begins to rise in the throat. John and Linda walk into the living room. They look like a normal family responding to a normal, tragic loss.

Linda sets a glass casserole dish down on the coffee table and immediately crosses the room. She sits down on the sofa and wraps her arms around my shoulders, pulling me into a fierce, desperate hug. She smells like vanilla extract, expensive wool, and crisp winter air.

The scent of a safe, idyllic childhood I never experienced. The body goes completely, terrifyingly rigid. I keep my arms locked around my knees.

I don't hug her back. "Chloe, sweetheart," Linda weeps softly into my hair. "I am so, so sorry."

I stare straight ahead at the muted television. The lungs feel packed with wet sand. Linda pulls back just enough to look at my face.

She reaches up, gently brushing a stray lock of dark hair behind an ear. "I know it feels like the end of the world right now," Linda whispers. "But it is a senseless tragedy, Chloe."

"That's all it is. Sometimes biology is just cruel. You have to remember that this is nobody's fault."

"Do you hear me? You did nothing wrong." Her lifeline wraps around the throat like a garrote.

Nobody's fault. Vision blurs. The pristine living room begins to tilt.

The smell of vanilla vanishes, violently overwritten by the phantom stench of cheap alcohol and rotting wood. If Linda knew the truth, she wouldn't be touching me. She is mourning a victim of a biological accident.

She has no idea she is hugging a monster. I am not a tragic, grieving mother. I am a coward who packed a pillowcase with clothes and climbed out a window, leaving a helpless infant behind with a predator to save my own skin.

I sacrificed Tyra to buy freedom. And now, the universe balances the ledger. It took Isabella to pay the debt.

It is entirely my fault. The guilt is so absolute and crushing the ribs might physically snap under the pressure. I am a poison.

I ruin everything I touch. "I need to lie down," I whisper, pulling away from Linda's touch. I stand up.

Legs shake, but the adrenaline of panic keeps them upright. I don't look at John. I don't look at the foil-covered dish on the table.

As I walk past Alex, he reaches out, his fingers gently catching my elbow. "Chloe," he murmurs, his voice breaking. "Please."

It takes every ounce of strength left in a shattered soul to gently, firmly pull the arm out of his grasp. One look, and the entire facade shatters. "I'm just tired, Alex," I lie.

I leave them standing in the living room—a portrait of a perfect, grieving family I permanently ruined. I walk up the stairs, my hand gripping the wooden banister like a lifeline. I go straight into the master bedroom, and I push the door closed.

Click. I throw the deadbolt, locking the normal, loving world out. The silence of the bedroom returns, and my eyes drift automatically toward the open door of the master closet.

The plastic bin is still up there on the highest shelf, hiding in the dark corner. Dr. Harris said navigate the complexity. Alex said the ghosts couldn't reach here.

They were both wrong. My ghost isn't chasing me; it is inside me. I walk slowly toward the closet, entirely surrendering to the descent.

14 THE EXTRACTOR

CHLOE

The air in the locked bedroom is entirely too thin. I press my back against the solid wooden door. Muffled, gentle cadences of Alex's voice drift upstairs, mingling with his parents'.

They are fixing a tragedy. They don't know they are trying to bandage a curse. I can't stay in this house.

The sheer, suffocating weight of their unconditional love is physically crushing the ribs. If I stay, the darkness will eventually leak out and wrap its hands around Alex's throat, just like it wrapped its hands around Isabella. I step away from the door.

I pull on a pair of rugged black boots, wrap myself in a thick wool coat, and slip out through the adjoining master bathroom, taking the back staircase down to the mudroom. I step out into the freezing winter. The cold is a physical shock, a sharp slap across the face that instantly snaps the lungs to attention.

I walk two blocks down the icy suburban sidewalk, shivering violently, and wait for my rideshare. Twenty minutes later, my boots hit the wet, salted pavement of the gallery district. I push the heavy glass door open.

Lila steps out from the back hallway, holding a delicate crystal glass of red wine. She stops walking the second she sees me in the entryway. Her piercing grey eyes sweep over the shivering frame.

She takes a slow sip of her wine, a sudden, predatory hunger gleaming in the light. "You look like absolute hell, Chloe," she says, her voice dropping into a smooth, approving purr. "Good."

It is the most honest thing anyone has said in four days. I unbutton my thick coat, letting it slide off my shoulders into a careless heap. I follow her down the long, narrow hallway to the private studio.

The room smells aggressively of turpentine, raw linseed oil, and metallic dust. An intoxicating, familiar poison. Lila picks up a thick, unsharpened stick of compressed charcoal.

She turns and holds it out. "Healing is for people who have something left to save," Lila says, her voice a sharp, commanding whip. "You and I both know that's not you, Chloe."

"You are a creature of the dark." She presses the charcoal directly into my trembling palm. "Stop playing house," she whispers fiercely.

"Take all of that grief, take all of that agonizing, suffocating guilt, and bleed it onto this canvas. Give me the monster." Fingers close around the charcoal.

I turn toward the towering white canvas. I don't think. I don't plan.

I just let the dam break. I raise my hand and slam the charcoal against the pristine white fabric. The sound of compressed ash dragging violently across the weave is a harsh, abrasive scream.

I don't draw a face. I don't draw a baby. I draw the cage.

I pull my arm down in a vicious, vertical slash. Then another. And another.

The black lines multiply, overlapping, growing thicker and denser. I draw frantic, jagged, furious strokes. I build the iron bars of the fence.

The claustrophobic, suffocating walls of the kitchenette. The inescapable reality of Tyra left inside. I press so hard the thick stick of charcoal snaps in half.

The sharp edge punctures the canvas, tearing small, jagged holes right through the fabric. I don't stop. I pick up the broken piece and keep going, locking the entire canvas behind a dense, impenetrable prison of heavy black vertical lines.

Black dust rains down, coating the hands, the wrists, the front of the grey sweater. Soot. The ashes of the yellow nursery.

I drop the crushed nub of charcoal. I turn to the cart and grab a solid metal tube of cadmium red oil paint. I don't reach for a brush.

I unscrew the cap and squeeze the thick, dense pigment directly into my palm. It feels cold, heavy, and horrifyingly wet. I step up to the canvas and press my paint-soaked hand directly into the center of the black bars.

I push hard, and I smear it violently across the charcoal. I drag my palm diagonally across the canvas, embedding the thick red oil into the weave of the fabric, aggressively slicing through the dark cage. It looks exactly like an open wound.

You leave things in the dark, the voice hisses in the mind. *You are the poison.* I squeeze more paint into my hands.

I slap them against the canvas, pulling the visceral, bloody crimson across the black lines in thick, textured streaks. I paint until the lungs burn. I paint until the pristine white canvas is completely obliterated by a chaotic, violent, terrifying storm of dense black ash and hand-smeared red.

Finally, the arms give out. I stumble backward, the chest heaving violently. I stare at the canvas.

The thick red paint drips slowly down the black charcoal bars. It is a mirror reflecting the absolute, undeniable truth of the soul. I am not Isabella's mother.

I am not Alex's wife. I am just the girl who ran away, permanently trapped behind those black, jagged bars. "It's horrifying," Lila breathes behind me.

"It is an absolute masterpiece, Chloe." She is right. The glass house was a lie.

I don't deserve to breathe the same air as the man who loved me. The infection must be permanently severed before it destroys him. I don't say a word to Lila.

I turn, I walk out of the studio, and head back out into the freezing, grey slush. Back to the house. Back to the closet.

It is time to open the velvet box, swallow the pills, and lock the door forever.

15 **THE DESCENT**

CHLOE

The ride back to the house dissolves into a freezing, grey blur. The icy driveway crunches beneath my boots. I push the front door open.

Alex paces the hardwood floor, his phone gripped tightly in his hand. He turns. He freezes.

I catch a glimpse of my reflection in the hallway mirror. A casualty of war. The brown face staring back is hollowed out.

My hands and forearms are stained with black charcoal dust. Visceral smears of cadmium red oil paint track across my grey sweater like fresh blood. Alex doesn't yell.

He slowly crosses the distance, his dark eyes brimming with a terrifying, helpless panic. He stops a foot away, his hands hovering in the air, too afraid to touch me after the rejection in the hospital.

"Chloe," he whispers, his voice trembling so violently it cracks. "Please. I can't fix this. I don't know how to fix this. Just... please tell me what to do. Let me in."

His desperate, shattered face offers no solutions. The architect has finally run out of blueprints. He is begging for a door, but he is standing in front of a sealed vault of poison.

No words come to me. I just offer a slow shake of my head. I sidestep past his hovering hands and retreat toward the stairs.

The staircase stretches upward, an impossible mountain. I drag myself up every step. I pull the solid master bathroom door shut, engaging the lock with a sharp snap.

The pristine white marble floor is spotless now, bleached and scrubbed clean of the blood I spilled days ago. I sink down, resting my back against the cool edge of the porcelain bathtub. My fingers, still coated in black ash, shake violently against the smooth glass of my phone screen.

I open the web browser. The cursor blinks steadily in the empty white search bar. First Name.

Last Name. State. My thumb hovers over the digital keyboard.

Just the letter T. One keystroke to find out if the daughter I left in the dark is still alive, or if Artie finally finished destroying her. Nausea rolls through my stomach, dense and sickening.

Typing the name makes it real. It means I have to look at the wreckage. The terrified, cowardly sixteen-year-old girl who climbed out that window is still here, completely paralyzed.

I couldn't save Tyra then, and I can't face her now. I click the screen off. Black glass.

I push myself up off the floor. I disengage the lock and step back out into the quiet hallway. At the top of the landing, the air shifts.

To my right, the solid white door of the spare bedroom is cracked open, just a fraction of an inch. I push the wood, and it swings wide. The "Morning Sunshine" yellow walls hit like a physical blow.

The track lighting is off, leaving the room submerged in the cool, grey shadows of the winter afternoon. The solid oak crib stands in the center. Pastel blankets, perfectly folded.

Tiny, soft-soled white shoes waiting on the closet shelf. Not a nursery. A perfectly preserved tomb.

I wrap my fingers around the thick wooden rail. I rest my forehead against the cold oak.

Rule number one, Artie's raspy, phantom voice echoes from the corners, smelling of scorched grease and stale cigarettes. *You don't get to leave. You don't get to have a new life.* "I know," I whisper into the empty room. "I know." I let go of the crib.

I turn away from the light and walk back down the hallway to the master bedroom. I head straight into the walk-in closet. No hesitation.

The absolute, terrifying clarity of my decision overpowers the fear. I drag the small wooden step stool across the floor. I climb up.

I reach deep into the highest, darkest corner of the top shelf and pull the large plastic storage bin down. I pop the lid off. I dig my hands through the thick winter blankets until my fingers brush the cold brass latch of the small wooden box.

I pull it free. I step down from the stool and press my back against the closet wall, surrounded by the hanging hems of Alex's tailored suits. I rest the velvet box on my lap.

Fourteen years shut. Fourteen years outrunning the memory. I slide my thumb under the brass latch and flip it open.

The hinges groan. Resting on the dark, faded velvet lining is the tiny, yellowed infant sock. The embroidered "T" on the ankle is frayed, faded by time, but undeniably real.

Absolute, physical proof of my unforgivable sin. My chest caves in. A ragged, animalistic sob tears its way out of my throat.

I press the sock frantically against my mouth, suffocating on the smell of old cotton and fourteen years of my suppressed grief. The toll is two lives. Tyra left to the monster, and the monster reaching through time to take Isabella.

I place the sock back into the velvet box. I reach deep into the pocket of my wool coat and pull out the small, amber plastic prescription bottle. Zolpidem.

I twist the child-proof cap and break the plastic seal with a sharp click. I tip the bottle, letting a dozen small, chalky white tablets spill into my trembling hand. They feel weightless.

A key to a door I never have to open again. I have no desire to die. Just a desperate need to stop existing.

To turn the deafening, screaming guilt off. To go back to the cage, where the rules are simple and the dark is absolute. I swallow the pills dry.

They scrape violently down the back of the throat, a harsh, bitter chalk, but I force them down. I pull my knees tightly to my chest, curling into a tiny, defensive ball on the closet floor. I wrap my arms securely around the velvet box, holding the yellowed sock flush against my heart.

I close my eyes. Within minutes, the edges of my reality blur. The cedar smell of the closet fades.

The soft cashmere brushing against my shoulder dissolves. The air grows dense and damp. The distinct, rhythmic squeak of a rusty hinge echoes.

The smell of cheap alcohol and ash returns. *Welcome home, Chloe*, the jagged voice whispers from the absolute black. I let out one final, shallow breath, and the dark pulls me completely under.

Hush now, little bird, don't you cry.
The dark is just a blanket in the sky.
Keep your voice low, keep your eyes tight,

We must be very quiet in the night.
If the monster hears you breathe,
He will never let us leave.

16 **THE UNEARTHING**

ALEX

The pharmacy bag crinkled loudly in the suffocating silence of the entryway. Alex stood on the woven mat just inside the front door, methodically kicking off his snow-covered boots. He had only been gone for forty-five minutes. He had driven slowly through the slush-filled streets, taking his time to pick up the strong pain medications the hospital had prescribed for Chloe. He wanted to give her the space she had silently, violently demanded when his parents were there.

He set his keys in the ceramic bowl on the console table. The metallic clink echoed down the long, shadowed hallway. "Chloe?" he called out, his voice a low, cautious rumble.

There was no answer. The house was entirely still, save for the low, rhythmic hum of the forced-air heater. Alex took off his thick wool coat and draped it over the banister. He carried the white paper pharmacy bag toward the kitchen, his eyes scanning the first floor. The living room was empty. The television was off. The glass casserole dish his mother had brought was sitting exactly where she had left it on the coffee table, untouched.

A tight, cold knot of unease began to form in the pit of his stomach. It wasn't the usual hyper-vigilance of a protective husband; it was the sharp, primal instinct of an animal sensing a shift in the air pressure right before a storm. He set the bag on the granite island and walked to the base of the stairs.

"Chloe, I've got your medication," he called out again, slightly louder this time.

Silence.

Alex took the stairs two at a time, his thudding footsteps echoing against the carpeted runner. He reached the second-floor landing and paused. The door to the nursery was cracked open, spilling a thin slice of grey afternoon light into the hallway. He moved past it, his jaw tightening, and stopped in front of the master bedroom. The door was ajar.

He pushed it open. The bed was perfectly made. The room was empty. But at the far end of the room, the door to the expansive walk-in closet was wide open, and the harsh, bright overhead track light was glaring.

Alex walked toward the closet. "Chloe, are you—"

The words died in his throat. Sitting on the floor, wedged deep into the corner beneath the hanging hems of his tailored suits, was Chloe. She was curled into a tight, defensive fetal position, her knees pulled flush against her chest. She was wearing her thick winter coat. Her dark hair was falling across her face, completely masking her expression.

"Chloe," Alex breathed, a sudden, terrifying spike of adrenaline flooding his system. He crossed the closet in two long strides and dropped to his knees beside her. He reached out, his large hands gripping her shoulders. She didn't flinch. She didn't pull away.

She was completely, terrifyingly limp. Her head rolled loosely to the side, exposing her ashen face. Her lips were tinted a faint, bruised blue.

"Hey. Hey, look at me," Alex commanded, his voice cracking as panic completely overtook his rational mind. He shook her shoulders, slightly harder this time. "Chloe, wake up. Open your eyes."

She didn't move. Alex's eyes darted frantically around the floor. Resting just inches from her knee was a small, amber plastic cylinder. The white child-proof cap was lying upside down on the rug. Zolpidem.

Alex snatched the bottle. It was completely empty.

"No," Alex choked out, a raw, animalistic sound of pure terror tearing its way out of his chest. "No, no, no. Chloe, stay with me!"

He dropped the bottle and violently dragged her out of the closet and onto the open floor of the bedroom. He pressed his trembling fingers hard against the side of her neck, searching for the carotid artery. Beneath his fingertips, he felt a pulse. It was there, but it was incredibly shallow and terrifyingly slow.

Alex pulled his phone from his pocket. His hands were shaking so violently he almost dropped it. He swiped the screen with a bloodless thumb and dialed 911.

"I need an ambulance," Alex shouted into the receiver the second the dispatcher answered, his voice echoing frantically off the bedroom walls. "My wife is unresponsive. She took a bottle of sedatives. She has a pulse, but she won't wake up. Please, you have to hurry!"

The next ten minutes dissolved into a chaotic, fragmented blur of absolute nightmare. The loud, authoritative pounding on the front door. The deafening wail of the sirens outside. The rush of cold winter air flooding the house as paramedics in thick navy-blue jackets swarmed up his stairs, their rugged boots tracking dirty grey slush into the pristine bedroom.

Alex was shoved backward, forced to stand helplessly against the wall while two strangers hovered over his wife. They shouted medical jargon over each other, shining harsh penlights into her unresponsive eyes, strapping a blood pressure cuff to her arm, and lifting her limp body onto a collapsible stretcher.

"We need to move, now," one of the paramedics barked, pulling the straps tight across her chest.

Alex followed them down the stairs, his mind completely fractured. He watched them load her into the back of the ambulance, the red and blue emergency lights flashing violently against the white snowbanks.

"You can't ride with us, sir. We have to work," the paramedic said, holding a hand up to stop him from climbing into the rig. "Follow us to Memorial. Do you have her ID and medical history?"

"Yes," Alex stammered blindly. "Yes, I'll get it. I'll be right behind you."

The ambulance doors slammed shut, and the large vehicle tore out of the driveway, the sirens screaming into the grey afternoon. Alex stood alone in the freezing driveway for a long, fractured moment. The world felt like it was spinning completely off its axis. He had lost his daughter, and now, he was losing his wife. The fortress he had built had utterly failed to protect them from the one thing he couldn't see: her own mind.

He spun around and ran back into the house, leaving the front door wide open. He sprinted up the stairs, taking them three at a time, entirely focused on packing a bag and getting to the hospital. He rushed back into the master bedroom, his boots crushing the discarded plastic wrappers the paramedics had left on the floor. He went straight to the closet to grab her purse and a clean set of clothes.

He stepped into the harsh glare of the closet light. He reached for the duffel bag on the bottom shelf, but his hand froze in mid-air. Sitting in the exact spot where Chloe had collapsed, half-hidden beneath the hem of a hanging wool sweater, was a small, dark object.

Alex slowly lowered himself to a crouch. It was a small, antique wooden box. The brass latch was flipped open, the hinges groaning slightly as he brushed it with his finger. Inside the box, resting on a bed of faded, dark velvet, was a tiny, yellowed infant's sock.

Alex stared at it. His analytical mind, shattered by panic just minutes before, suddenly snapped back into a state of cold, razor-sharp clarity. He reached out and picked up the sock. The cotton was stiff with age. Embroidered into the ankle with faded dark thread was a single, undeniable letter: T.

It wasn't Isabella's. Isabella had never worn clothes. And Chloe had never bought anything antique or yellowed; everything in the nursery was pristine, brand new, and pastel.

Alex looked back down at the floor. Lying just a few inches from the wooden box, shoved partially under a pair of shoes, was Chloe's thick leather journal. The binding was cracked. It had fallen open when the paramedics dragged her out of the closet.

Alex picked it up. His eyes locked onto the jagged, frantic handwriting scrawled across the lined paper in thick, smudged black ink.

I try not to look in the crib when she cries. If I don't look, I can pretend she is just mine. But the shape of her jaw is getting sharper. The darkness in her eyes is too deep. He stands over the crib for hours, just watching her breathe, smiling that cold, dead smile. He knows. Every time I hold her, I feel like I am holding a piece of him. I love her, but I am so terrified she is going to grow up and look exactly like the monster.

I left her in the dark. I climbed out the window, and I left her in the cage. He was right. Artie was always right. I am a monster. I sacrificed Tyra to save myself, and now the universe has taken Isabella to balance the debt.

Alex stopped breathing. The words didn't make sense. They broke every single law of physics and reality that his marriage was built upon. He read the paragraphs again. And then a third time.

Tyra. Artie. The cage.

A profound, terrifying chill rushed through Alex's veins, completely replacing the frantic heat of his panic. The devastating grief of the last four days instantly hardened into something entirely different. It hardened into a cold, relentless, terrifying focus.

Chloe wasn't running from an abstract feeling. She wasn't fighting a generalized trauma. She was running from a specific place. She was running from a specific man. And she had left a daughter behind.

Alex slowly closed the leather journal. He looked at the tiny, yellowed sock in his hand. The architect who built nurseries was gone. Standing in the harsh light of the closet was a man who suddenly realized that the foundation of his entire life was a lie, and he was staring directly at the only two puzzle pieces he had.

He placed the sock back into the velvet box and put the box into his coat pocket. He gripped the leather journal tightly in his right hand. He turned and walked out of the closet, heading for the hospital, ready to begin the hunt.

17 THE CATALYST FOR THE HUNT

ALEX

The fluorescent lights of the intensive care waiting room buzzed with a low, mechanical hum. It was a sterile, unforgiving sound. Alex sat perfectly still in a rigid plastic chair, his thick winter coat draped over his knees. His dark eyes were fixed on the scuffed linoleum floor.

"Mr. Mercer?" Alex looked up. A tired ICU physician in green scrubs stood a few feet away, holding a digital tablet.

"We pumped her stomach," the doctor said softly, his voice carrying the practiced, deep empathy of a man who delivered bad news for a living. "Physically, the sedatives are clearing her system. Her vitals are stabilizing. But neurologically... she isn't waking up."

Alex's jaw tightened. "Explain that."

"It appears to be a psychogenic coma," the doctor explained, stepping slightly closer. "It is a rare, severe dissociative state. Her brain has experienced a trauma so profound, so completely overwhelming, that it essentially built a wall and shut the doors. She is physically capable of waking up, Alex. But her mind is refusing to return to reality. She is hiding."

The doctor waited, his posture braced as if expecting Alex to break down, to yell, or to bury his face in his hands. Alex did none of those things. He didn't cry. He just stared at the empty space where the doctor had been standing long after the man walked away. *She is hiding.* Alex slowly reached into the deep pocket of his coat. His fingers brushed against the small, antique wooden box, but he bypassed it, wrapping his hand around the cracked leather journal. He pulled it out and set it on his lap. He had never opened it before. For the three years they had been together, he had treated this book as her sacred, private ground. But the woman he loved was currently trapped behind a wall in her own mind, and this book was the only door left. He opened the thick cover.

The very first thing that hit him was the sheer violence of her handwriting. It wasn't the flowing, artistic script she used for grocery lists or thank-you cards. The words were jagged, frantic, and pressed so deeply into the paper that the ink bled through the pages. Some entries were smudged with charcoal; others were warped by dried tear stains. He turned to an entry dated six months ago, right after they had finished painting the nursery.

He thinks the yellow paint covers the rot. He thinks the locks on the doors keep the monsters outside. I smile at him, and I tell him I feel safe, but I am a liar. I am a walking infection. Every time he kisses me, I am terrified I am going to pass the disease to him. The ghost is standing in the corner of the nursery, and she is staring at me.

Alex felt a cold stone drop into his stomach. He turned the page, the dry paper rasping loudly in the quiet waiting room. He moved forward in time, to the week Isabella died.

The blood on the marble floor wasn't a medical complication. It was a collection. The universe doesn't let you run away from a debt. It just waits until you have something worth taking.

Alex stopped breathing. His hands began to tremble slightly, the leather binding creaking under his tightening grip. He had spent months trying to comfort her, trying to tell her that biology was just cruel, but she hadn't been mourning a miscarriage. She had been accepting a punishment. He flipped to the very last page. The ink here was fresh, deeply smeared, and frantic.

The lock is broken. Artie is in the hallway. I can smell the scorched grease and the damp wood. Rule number one: you don't get to have a new life. I left her in the dark. I climbed out that window and I left

Tyra in the cage. I am a monster. I sacrificed her to save myself, and now the dark has taken Isabella to balance the ledger. I have to go back to the dark. It is the only place I belong.

Alex stared at the words until they blurred. He slowly reached into his other pocket and pulled out the velvet box. He flipped the brass latch. He looked at the tiny, yellowed infant's sock with the faded pink "T" embroidered on the ankle. The pieces of the nightmare finally snapped together, forming a horrifying, undeniable picture.

Fourteen years ago, Chloe had arrived in the city. She was sixteen years old. The story she had told him—the story she had told everyone—was that she was a chronic runaway fleeing a string of abusive, nameless foster homes. She had claimed she was completely alone in the world until Nina and Jason, wealthy gallery owners, took her in, gave her a home, and paid for her schooling. But a sixteen-year-old runaway didn't have a preserved infant's sock hidden in a velvet box. A runaway didn't write about climbing out a window, leaving someone named Tyra behind in a cage to save herself. His wife wasn't a runaway. She was an escapee. And she had left a child behind.

Alex closed the journal. He didn't walk through the double doors to sit by her hospital bed. He knew sitting in the sterile room holding her hand wouldn't save her. She wasn't fighting a medical anomaly; she was fighting a man named Artie. And the only way to wake his wife up was to drag that man out of the dark and destroy him. If Chloe's history was a desperate lie, there were only two people in the world who possessed the influence to help her bury it. The gatekeepers. Alex stood up. He shoved the box and the journal back into his coat pocket, turned his back on the ICU, and walked out into the freezing winter night.

Thirty minutes later, Alex's large SUV idled in the driveway of a sprawling, immaculate suburban estate. Nina and Jason's home was a picture of comfortable, oblivious wealth. Warm, inviting light spilled from the large bay windows, illuminating the pristine, snow-covered lawn. It was a house completely untouched by the nightmare Alex was currently living in. He cut the engine. He marched up the manicured stone pathway. He reached the solid front door and didn't bother with the elegant brass doorbell. He raised his fist and pounded on the wood—three loud, authoritative strikes that echoed loudly in the quiet neighborhood.

A moment later, the deadbolt clicked. The door swung open, revealing Jason in a cashmere sweater. The older man looked mildly annoyed until his eyes locked onto Alex's face. "Alex?" Jason blinked, entirely taken aback. "What are you doing here? We heard the ambulance at your place on the scanner, Nina has been trying to call—"

Alex didn't wait for an invitation. He stepped forward, breaching the threshold, forcing Jason to take a hurried step backward into the foyer. Alex was a formidable man, but he spent his life consciously softening his edges to make the people around him feel safe. Standing in their entryway, letting the freezing winter wind whip through the open door, he stopped softening. He let his sheer size and furious grief take over the room.

"Jason? Who is it?" Nina's voice called out from the living room. She hurried around the corner, stopping short when she saw Alex. Her hands flew to her mouth, her eyes welling with immediate tears. "Oh, Alex. We heard the sirens. We were so terrified. Is it Chloe? Is she alright?" She rushed forward, reaching her arms out to pull him into a comforting embrace.

Alex sidestepped her. The movement was so cold, and so utterly devoid of his usual warmth, that Nina froze in her tracks. He walked past her, stepping down into their sunken, impeccably decorated living room. He stopped in front of the expensive mahogany coffee table. He reached into his coat pocket and pulled out the velvet box. He dropped it onto the wood. *Clack.* He pulled out the leather journal and tossed it down next to the box. *Thud.*

"Chloe is in the intensive care unit," Alex said. His voice was a low, terrifyingly calm rumble. "She swallowed a bottle of sedatives. She is currently in a psychogenic coma because the guilt of her past finally broke her mind."

Nina let out a sharp, horrifying gasp, her hand pressing hard against her chest. "Oh my god. A coma? Alex, the miscarriage... the trauma of losing Isabella—"

"This has nothing to do with Isabella," Alex interrupted smoothly. His dark eyes locked onto Nina. "It has to do with Tyra."

The color drained entirely from Nina's face. It wasn't a subtle shift. It was an instant, catastrophic physical reaction. Her mouth opened slightly, but no sound came out. Her eyes darted frantically toward Jason.

"Chloe has an active imagination," Jason stammered quickly, stepping forward, his hands raised in a placating gesture. "You know how she is, Alex. When the night terrors get bad, she hallucinates. She invents names, she invents scenarios—"

"Don't," Alex warned, his voice dropping a full octave, vibrating with a dangerous, lethal edge. He pointed a long finger at the velvet box on the table. "You don't get to lie to me, Jason. I found that box hidden in the ceiling of my closet. I just read fourteen years of her agony in that journal. Chloe didn't run away from a bad foster home. She ran away from a cage. And she left an infant behind."

Nina let out a broken, jagged sob, covering her face with her hands. Alex took a slow, deliberate step toward Jason, backing the older man up against the edge of a leather armchair. "You're wealthy gallery owners. You took a feral, traumatized sixteen-year-old girl off the street and put her through private art school. Why? Because you found her sleeping in an alley with that velvet box in her backpack? Did she confess what she did, and you decided her talent was worth the cover-up?"

"You don't understand!" Nina cried out, dropping her hands from her face, her pristine suburban mask completely shattering. "She was just a child, Alex! When we found her, she was half-starved, screaming in her sleep every single night about the dark. We couldn't go to the police! If we reported her, she would have been sent right back into the system. She would have been sent back to him!"

"Who is he?" Alex demanded, his dark eyes burning with an unyielding fire. "Who is Artie? And where is the cage?"

"Please," Jason pleaded, his voice cracking as he stepped sideways, trying to physically put himself between Alex's wrath and his weeping wife. "We swore to her, Alex. We swore on our lives we would never say his name. If you go looking for him, you are going to get her killed! He doesn't even know she survived!"

"I am going to ask you one last time," Alex roared, the sudden, violent volume of his voice shaking the glass in the bay windows. "Give me the name!"

Jason flinched violently. The pressure was too much. The secret they had guarded for fourteen years buckled and snapped under the crushing weight of Alex's focus. "Arthur Vance!" Jason shouted back, his face pale and slick with sweat. "His name is Arthur Vance! He lives in Michigamee County. Now please, Alex, I am begging you, leave it alone!"

The name hung in the air, echoing off the high ceilings of the living room. Arthur Vance. Michigamee County. Alex's jaw set. The ghost haunting his wife finally had a name and a location. A name meant it was a man. And a man could be broken. He didn't argue. He didn't ask them for permission, and he didn't ask for their help. Alex reached down, picked up the leather journal and the velvet box, and slid them back into his coat pocket. He turned his back on their terrified faces, walked out the front door, and stepped into the freezing night to begin the hunt.

18 THE DEAD END

ALEX

Alex unlocked the front door of his home, stepping out of the freezing wind and into the entryway. He pushed the solid oak door shut, the deadbolts sliding into place with a series of loud, metallic thuds. The house was completely silent. He stood on the woven mat for a long time, listening to the low, rhythmic hum of the forced-air heater. He had spent years designing this house, reinforcing the doors, upgrading the glass, and perfecting the security system. It was built to be an impenetrable sanctuary for his wife. But standing in the dark hallway, listening to the absolute quiet, it didn't feel like a sanctuary. It felt like an empty vault.

He walked slowly down the hall, bypassing the darkened living room and the kitchen. He passed the base of the stairs, refusing to look up toward the second floor where the yellow nursery sat untouched. He went straight to his home office at the back of the house and pushed the door open. It was a dark, masculine room lined with dark bookshelves and a broad oak desk. He walked over to the desk and reached up, clicking on the brass reading lamp. A pool of warm, yellow light spilled across the polished wood. Alex took off his winter coat, draped it over the back of his leather chair, and sat down. He reached into his pocket. He pulled out the small velvet box and set it gently in the center of the light. He pulled out Chloe's cracked leather journal and placed it right beside the box.

He reached out and tapped the spacebar on his keyboard. The three monitors mounted above his desk flared to life, casting a cold, bluish glow across his exhausted, dark brown face. He opened a web browser. His hands hovered over the keys for a moment. He was about to cross a line he could never uncross, violating the protective boundary he had always maintained around Chloe's past. He pressed his lips into a tight line, completely surrendering to the necessity of it, and typed the name: *Arthur Vance*. He added the only other piece of the puzzle he had: *Michigamee County*. He pressed enter.

Alex leaned forward, his dark eyes scanning the cascade of search results. He expected to find something immediately—a public directory, a news article, a social media profile. But as he scrolled down the page, his brow furrowed in frustration. There was nothing. Arthur Vance was a complete ghost. Alex shifted his strategy. If a sixteen-year-old girl climbed out of a window and vanished into the freezing winter fourteen years ago, there had to be a record of her absence. A girl doesn't just cease to exist without leaving a ripple.

He accessed the digitized archives of the local county newspapers, setting the search parameters to the exact year Chloe had arrived in Detroit. He typed in keywords: *Runaway. Missing teen. Search party. Michigamee.* He hit enter. Zero results found. He opened a new tab and hacked his way through the public-facing portals of the state police missing persons database. He combed through the legacy files of unsolved runaway cases in the northern part of the state. None of them were Chloe.

Alex slowly pulled his hands away from the keyboard. The realization washed over him like a wave of ice water. There were no newspaper articles. There had never been a search party in the woods. Arthur Vance had never reported her missing. Vance hadn't called the police because Vance couldn't risk the police asking questions. He had simply let her vanish, keeping whatever secrets remained locked behind his doors.

Alex looked down at the velvet box. He flipped the brass latch open and stared at the tiny, yellowed infant's sock resting on the dark fabric. His thumb gently brushed the faded pink thread of the letter "T". *Tyra.* His analytical mind began to process the math, and the sheer weight of the numbers made his chest physically ache. Chloe had run away fourteen years ago. If she had left an infant behind in that dark, isolated cabin... that child wasn't a baby anymore. Tyra was fourteen years old.

Five thousand, one hundred and ten days trapped in the dark with a man Chloe considered a monster. The crushing, suffocating reality of what his wife had been carrying all these years finally settled over him. Alex rubbed his hands aggressively over his exhausted eyes. He took a deep, jagged breath and forced the grief back down. Anger was a much more useful tool right now.

He moved to his right monitor and logged directly into the Michigamee County Assessor's public database. He typed *Arthur Vance* into the property owner field. A single line of text appeared. It was a scanned, yellowing piece of paper—a delinquent tax notice dated fourteen years ago. A sprawling, sixty-acre plot of forested land registered to Arthur Vance had been flagged for seizure. But the land hadn't been seized. Right after Chloe's escape, the deed had been transferred. The name Arthur Vance was wiped from the county registry.

Instead, the current deed listed the owner as a blind corporate entity: Vance Holdings LLC. Alex clicked on the parcel. The physical address was entirely redacted. There were no GPS coordinates, only rural lot numbers that meant nothing without the master county grid map. The monster wasn't just a chaotic drunk living in a shack. He was deeply paranoid, and he treated his land like a sovereign territory. He had deliberately buried his fortress in corporate paperwork.

Alex hit a dead end. He couldn't hack a physical location that wasn't digitized. But as he scanned the LLC registration, his eyes locked onto a single, vulnerable detail. Vance Holdings LLC had a registered agent. A proxy whose job was to pay the annual property taxes and keep the state blind to whatever was happening in the woods. *Marcus Heller, Attorney at Law.* Alex looked at the address listed for the lawyer. It wasn't in Michigamee. It was a strip mall in Southfield, just thirty minutes away. Alex closed his laptop. He didn't need to be a hacker anymore. He was a corporate risk manager, and he was about to go to work.

19 **THE PAPER TRAIL**

ALEX

The office of Marcus Heller, Attorney at Law, was nestled between a failing dry cleaner and a discount liquor store in a decaying Southfield strip mall. The blinds were drawn, coated in a thick layer of yellowed dust. Alex parked his pristine, black SUV directly in front of the glass door. He didn't look like a grieving husband. He had armored himself. He was wearing a tailored, charcoal-grey bespoke suit, a crisp white shirt, and a steel-faced chronograph watch that cost more than the lawyer's car. He looked exactly like what he was: an apex predator from the financial district.

Alex pushed the glass door open. The bell above the frame gave a pathetic, muted jingle. The interior smelled of stale cigarette smoke and cheap coffee. Behind a cluttered, faux-wood laminate desk sat a balding man in a rumpled dress shirt. Marcus Heller looked up from his computer screen, his eyes immediately dropping to the cut of Alex's suit and the expensive watch. Heller sat up straighter, smelling money.

"Can I help you?" Heller asked, offering a greasy, practiced smile.

Alex didn't smile back. He walked to the desk, his imposing frame dominating the cramped, poorly lit room. He didn't sit in the cracked leather guest chair. He reached into his tailored breast pocket, pulled out a thick, banded stack of hundred-dollar bills, and dropped it directly onto the center of the desk. Ten thousand dollars in crisp, uncirculated cash.

Heller's eyes practically bulged out of his skull. He stared at the money, licking his dry lips. "What is this?"

"A transaction," Alex said, his voice cold, smooth, and utterly devoid of emotion. "You are the registered proxy for an entity called Vance Holdings LLC. I need the exact GPS coordinates and the physical property deed for the sixty-acre parcel in Michigamee County."

Heller's greasy smile instantly vanished. He pulled his hands back from the desk as if the money were on fire. The color drained from his face. "I don't know what you're talking about," Heller stammered, his eyes darting toward the door. "Client information is strictly confidential. I suggest you take your money and leave before I call the police."

Alex didn't move. He leaned over the desk, placing his broad, solid hands flat against the laminate wood. He looked directly into Heller's eyes, dropping the temperature in the room by ten degrees.

"Let me explain exactly who I am, Mr. Heller," Alex said, his voice a low, lethal hum. "I manage catastrophic risk for a multi-billion dollar financial firm. I destroy people for a living. I know you process cash payments for a man who lives off the grid. I know you hide his assets from the IRS. If you pick up that phone, I won't kill you. I will simply freeze every bank account you have, flag your firm for federal tax evasion, and ensure you spend the rest of your life answering to a federal grand jury."

Heller swallowed hard, a bead of sweat breaking out on his receding hairline. Alex tapped the stack of cash with his index finger.

"Or," Alex continued softly, "you can open your filing cabinet, hand me the deed, and take the ten thousand dollars. Arthur Vance will never know you gave it to me, because Arthur Vance is never going to speak to another human being again."

Heller stared at the towering, terrifyingly calm man in front of him. He looked at the cash. He weighed the threat of a feral hermit three hundred miles away against the immediate, corporate executioner standing in his office. Heller's hand trembled as he reached out and slid the stack of hundreds into his open briefcase. Without a word, the lawyer stood up, walked to a locked metal filing cabinet in the corner, and pulled out a single, thin manila folder. He placed it on the desk and slid it across to Alex.

"He's crazy," Heller whispered, his voice shaking. "I just pay the taxes, so the county doesn't go up there. Whatever you're looking for... the man is a ghost. He's armed to the teeth, and he doesn't let anyone onto that land."

"I'm not asking for permission," Alex said flatly. He opened the folder. Sitting on top of the legal jargon was a printed satellite map with a stark, red boundary line drawn around a sixty-acre square. At the bottom of the page, printed in bold black ink, were the exact longitudinal and latitudinal coordinates.

Alex closed the folder. He turned his back on the trembling lawyer and walked out into the freezing Michigan morning. He climbed into his SUV and locked the doors. He placed the folder on the passenger seat and opened his tablet. He punched the exact coordinates into his high-resolution satellite software. The map on the screen shifted rapidly. It pulled away from the city, plunging deep into miles of dense, unbroken, dark green pine forest in the absolute middle of nowhere.

The satellite image slowed, resolving into a sharp, top-down view. Alex stopped breathing. Sitting in the dead center of the dense timber was a large, man-made dirt clearing. In the middle of the clearing was a rusted, metal-roofed structure. And tracing the absolute perimeter of the clearing, forming a perfect, inescapable square around the structure, was a high, reinforced fence.

Alex zoomed in. The image became slightly grainy, but the details held. Parked in the dirt, just a few yards from the metal-roofed bunker, was a battered pickup truck. The property wasn't abandoned. Arthur Vance was still there. And Tyra was trapped inside.

Alex closed the tablet. His jaw set into a rigid, unbreakable line. He put the SUV in drive, turned his back on the strip mall, and headed home to arm himself for the dark.

20 THE THRESHOLD

ALEX

Alex pushed his chair back from the desk. The thick leather groaned in the quiet office. The three computer monitors still glowed with the stark, grainy satellite image of the metal-roofed structure sitting in the Michigamee forest, but Alex was done looking at screens. The digital hunt was over. It was time to deal with the physical reality of the cage. He stood up and walked to the deep closet at the back of his office. He pushed a row of tailored wool suits aside, exposing the solid steel floor safe bolted into the foundation.

He knelt on the hardwood. His fingers, usually accustomed to typing out precise financial algorithms, gripped the cold metal dial. He spun in the combination. *Click.* He pulled the solid steel door open. Alex reached inside and bypassed the stack of legal documents and passports. He reached all the way to the back and pulled out a dark canvas tactical duffel bag. He stood up and dropped the bag onto his desk. He wasn't packing for a business trip. He was packing for an extraction.

He methodically loaded the duffel. Rugged, insulated winter boots. A thick, non-reflective black parka rated for sub-zero temperatures. A high-lumen tactical flashlight. A thick coil of nylon rope. A trauma kit. Finally, he walked back to the safe and pulled out a lockbox. He keyed it open and lifted out a large-caliber, matte-black handgun.

Alex stood in the warm, yellow light of his reading lamp, holding the cold steel in his hands. He was a man who solved problems with intellect and capital, but looking at the weapon, he accepted a terrifying truth: reason would not work on a monster. Arthur Vance didn't negotiate. He pressed the magazine release. He checked the rounds, the metallic clack echoing sharply in the silent room. He shoved the gun into a stiff leather holster, packed three extra magazines into the canvas bag, and zipped it shut.

His cell phone, resting on the edge of the desk, suddenly began to vibrate. The screen illuminated the dark room. *Incoming Call: Jason.* Alex stared at the name for a long moment. He reached out and accepted the call, putting it on speaker.

"Alex?" Jason's voice was thin, trembling with a frantic, exhausted panic. "Alex, please tell me you're still at home. Nina is beside herself. We've been talking, and we want to help you figure this out—"

"I know exactly where the Michigamee compound is, Jason," Alex interrupted. His voice was a low, emotionless rumble, entirely devoid of mercy. "I saw the lawyer. I have the deed. I am leaving now."

"No, you can't!" Jason gasped, the panic escalating into pure terror. "You don't understand the kind of man Arthur Vance is! If you go up there, he will kill you, Alex. He's a paranoid survivalist. You are going to get yourself killed, and you are going to drag all of us down with you!"

"Listen to me very carefully," Alex said, his dark eyes fixed entirely on the blank wall of his office. "If you try to warn him, or if you interfere with this in any way, I won't just go to the police about your fourteen-year cover-up. I will destroy your life. Am I understood?"

"Alex, please, be rational—"

Alex ended the call. He didn't put the phone in his pocket. He dropped it onto the desk. He wouldn't need a cell phone where he was going.

Forty minutes later, Alex pushed open the solid wooden door of the Intensive Care Unit. The room was dim, illuminated only by the rhythmic, pulsing glow of the heart monitor. Chloe looked impossibly small in the center of the mechanical hospital bed. Her dark hair was fanned out across the stark white pillow. Her face was pale, serene, and entirely absent. She was trapped behind a wall in her own mind, fighting a ghost he couldn't see.

Alex walked to the edge of the bed and reached into the pocket of his coat. He pulled out the tiny, yellowed infant's sock with the faded pink "T" embroidered on the ankle. He reached out and took Chloe's limp, freezing hand. He gently opened her fingers, pressed the soft cotton fabric against her palm, and carefully curled her hand closed around it. He covered her hand with his own, holding it tightly for a long, quiet moment. He leaned down, pressing his face close to hers. He could smell the sterile hospital bleach, but beneath it, the faint, lingering scent of her lavender shampoo.

"You don't have to hide anymore," Alex whispered fiercely into her ear. "I'm going into the dark, Chloe. I'm going to bring the rest of you back."

He pressed a long, lingering kiss to her forehead. Alex turned around, walked out of the ICU, and didn't look back.

Dawn was just beginning to break, casting a cold, bruised purple light over the city as Alex climbed into his large SUV. He tossed the canvas duffel bag into the passenger seat and started the engine. He merged onto the northbound interstate, gripping the leather steering wheel. As the miles ticked by, the civilized world completely fell away. The towering glass skyscrapers and the chaotic, familiar noise of the city faded in the rearview mirror. The concrete gave way to desolate, snow-covered highways. The dense, isolating, and terrifyingly silent pine forests of northern Michigan rose up to swallow the road ahead.

The hunt had officially begun.

21 **THE EDGE OF THE MAP**

ALEX

By mid-afternoon, the pale winter sun had surrendered entirely to a dark, bruised overcast, turning the sky the color of wet iron. The wide, salted interstates of the lower peninsula were long gone. For the last two hours, the paved highway had steadily narrowed, degrading into a treacherous, ice-slicked two-lane road. Towering, snow-laden pine trees flanked the asphalt on both sides, pressing inward like a suffocating, dark green wall.

Alex glanced down at the glowing digital console on his dashboard. The GPS map stuttered. The blue line indicating his route froze, pixelated, and vanished entirely, replaced by a blank grey grid. Beside it, the cellular service indicator blinked once and dropped to a definitive *No Service*. He was officially off the grid.

Alex didn't panic. He reached over to the passenger seat and picked up the physical topographic maps he had printed in his office. He traced his finger along the contour lines, matching the shape of the frozen river to his right with the ink on the paper. He was getting close.

Suddenly, the blinding flash of red and blue strobe lights erupted in his rearview mirror. Alex's jaw tightened. He looked up. A battered, salt-stained Michigamee County Sheriff's cruiser was riding his bumper, the siren wailing a short, aggressive burst over the howling wind. There was no shoulder on the narrow, ice-slicked road. Alex smoothly decelerated, pulling his large SUV as far to the right as he safely could, his tires crunching into the deep snowbank.

He shifted into park. He didn't reach for the canvas duffel bag on the passenger seat. He rolled his window down, letting the freezing, biting wind whip into the heated cabin. In the side mirror, a heavy-set deputy in a thick winter uniform stepped out of the cruiser. He unclipped the safety strap on his holster as he walked slowly toward the SUV. He didn't look like a man making a routine traffic stop. He looked like a man who knew exactly who he was pulling over.

Jason. Alex realized it instantly. The coward hadn't called Vance; he had called the local cops to stop Alex from reaching the compound and exposing the fourteen-year-old secret. The deputy stopped slightly behind the driver's side pillar, keeping himself out of the direct line of sight.

"License and registration," the deputy demanded, his breath pluming in the freezing air.

Alex reached into his coat pocket slowly, telegraphing his movements, and handed the laminated cards out the window.

The deputy looked at the Detroit address. His eyes narrowed. "Long way from home, Mr. Mercer. We got a call from a concerned party downstate. Said a man matching your description was heading up here in a highly agitated state. Said you might be a danger to yourself or others."

"My wife is in the hospital," Alex said. His voice was perfectly calm, an icy, unwavering baritone. "I'm driving up to our family cabin to retrieve some of her belongings."

"Is that right?" The deputy rested his heavy, gloved hand on the butt of his sidearm. He leaned slightly forward, peering into the back seat of the SUV. "Where's this cabin?"

"Off County Road 44," Alex lied smoothly, naming a paved route twenty miles in the opposite direction of the Vance property.

The deputy didn't buy it. "Step out of the vehicle, Mr. Mercer. Keep your hands where I can see them."

Alex looked at the deputy in the side mirror. If he stepped out of the car, the deputy would search the vehicle. He would find the tactical gear, the rope, and the large-caliber handgun. Alex would be detained, sitting in a rural holding cell while Arthur Vance remained untouched in the woods. Tyra didn't have time for Alex to be arrested.

"Deputy," Alex said, his voice dropping an octave, losing the polite veneer of a civilian. "I am going to ask you to hand my license back. I am going to roll my window up, and I am going to drive away."

The deputy scoffed, taking a step back and drawing his weapon halfway out of the holster. "Step out of the damn car, or I will pull you out."

"You have no cell service out here," Alex said, his dark eyes locking onto the deputy through the side mirror. "Your radio is bouncing off a repeater that barely reaches the station. If you draw that weapon, you are going to be standing alone on an icy road with a man who has absolutely nothing left to lose. And I promise you, I will not be the one who freezes to death out here today."

The air in the cabin grew incredibly tense. It wasn't a threat; it was an absolute, terrifying statement of fact. Alex wasn't a criminal, but in that moment, the apex predator from the financial district merged entirely with a desperate, grieving husband. The resulting energy was lethal.

The deputy stared at Alex's reflection. He saw the cold, dead certainty in the man's eyes. This wasn't a panicked civilian. This was a man willing to burn the forest down. The deputy's grip loosened on his sidearm. He swallowed hard, the bravado evaporating in the freezing wind. He practically threw the license and registration back through the open window.

"County Road 44 is twenty miles back the way you came," the deputy said, his voice tight. "Turn around. If I catch you anywhere near the logging roads, I'll bring the whole department down on you."

"Understood," Alex said.

He rolled the window up, shifted the SUV into drive, and pulled away from the snowbank, leaving the deputy standing on the frozen asphalt. Alex didn't turn around. He drove five miles deeper into the dark, suffocating pines, watching the cruiser fade in the rearview mirror until he reached the unmarked dirt turnoff. He shifted the SUV into four-wheel drive and cut the wheel hard into the woods.

The drive became a slow, brutal crawl. The forest immediately swallowed the vehicle. The trees pressed in so tightly that their thick, frozen branches scraped against the doors with a high-pitched screech. The isolation was total and absolute. He drove for three miles. Finally, the dense wall of pine trees ahead began to thin. The pale, grey light of the open sky filtered through the branches.

Alex didn't drive all the way to the clearing. He steered the large SUV deep into a thick cluster of evergreens, burying the vehicle in the shadows where it couldn't be seen from the road. He shifted into park and killed the engine. The silence of the Michigamee woods rushed in, deafening and profound.

Alex reached into the passenger seat and unzipped the dark canvas duffel bag. He pulled out the large-caliber handgun and strapped the cold leather holster securely to his hip. He pulled the thick, black parka over his shoulders, zipping it all the way to his chin. He grabbed his tactical flashlight and shoved two extra magazines into his deep coat pockets. He opened the door and stepped down into the knee-deep snow.

Alex hiked the final quarter mile on foot, his rugged boots breaking the pristine crust of the snow with measured, deliberate, silent steps. The air was so cold it burned his lungs, but his heart beat in a slow, perfectly controlled rhythm. He reached the very edge of the woods and stopped, crouching behind the trunk of an ancient, frozen oak tree. He looked through the low-hanging branches.

Fifty yards away, sitting in the dead center of a vast dirt clearing, was the rusted, metal-roofed bunker. And rising out of the frozen ground, forming a perfect, inescapable square around the structure, was a ten-foot-tall, reinforced steel perimeter fence.

Alex stared at the rusted metal wire. It was exactly as Chloe had painted it. The cage was real. And Alex had finally arrived.

22 **INSIDE THE CAGE**

ALEX

Alex knelt in the knee-deep snow at the edge of the tree line, his breath pluming in the freezing air. Fifty yards away, the rusted, ten-foot perimeter fence loomed like a jagged scar against the pale grey sky. He studied the clearing with the cold, methodical precision of a man who spent his life assessing risk. There were no guard dogs pacing the frozen dirt. There were no security cameras mounted to the eaves of the metal-roofed bunker.

Arthur Vance didn't need modern security. He relied entirely on the absolute, crushing isolation of the Michigamee woods to keep his secrets buried.

Alex unzipped the canvas duffel bag. He bypassed the extra ammunition and pulled out a pair of large, industrial bolt cutters. He stood up, drew the large-caliber handgun from his hip holster, and stepped out of the shadow of the pines. He crossed the clearing quickly, his boots crunching softly against the frozen earth. When he reached the main gate, he holstered his weapon and gripped the bolt cutters. A thick, rusted chain and a thick brass padlock secured the swinging doors.

Alex aligned the steel jaws over the hasp of the lock. He engaged his broad shoulders and squeezed the handles together with everything he had. *Snap.* The sharp, metallic crack echoed like a gunshot in the silent clearing. Alex froze, his hand dropping to his weapon, his dark eyes scanning the tree line and the bunker. Nothing moved. The only sound was the wind howling through the evergreens. He pulled the severed lock free, unwound the chain, and slipped inside the perimeter.

He drew his gun again, holding it steady in a two-handed grip as he approached the bunker. The structure was long, low, and completely devoid of windows on the ground floor. It looked less like a house and more like a tomb. Alex reached the solid, reinforced wooden front door. He reached out with his left hand, expecting resistance, and turned the rusted iron knob.

It clicked, and the door swung inward with a low groan. It wasn't locked. The realization sent a cold spike of dread straight down Alex's spine. Vance didn't lock the outside world out. He only locked the inside world in.

Alex stepped over the threshold, bringing his weapon up as he breached the dark interior. The air inside hit him like a physical blow. It was thick, stagnant, and suffocating. It smelled exactly like the frantic, jagged words in Chloe's journal—scorched grease, damp, rotting wood, and unwashed wool. It was the scent of absolute despair.

He moved methodically through the dim, cluttered space, his tactical boots silent on the filthy floorboards. He swept the crude living area, scanning the overturned chairs and the trash-littered corners. Empty. He pivoted into the small kitchenette. The sink was piled high with rusted, unwashed cast-iron pans.

Alex paused, his eyes locking onto the large woodstove sitting in the corner of the room. He stepped closer and pulled his left glove off. He held his bare hand a few inches from the black iron. It was radiating intense, blistering heat.

Alex's analytical mind instantly calculated the terrifying deficit he was facing. Woodstoves in this kind of sub-zero temperature burned through fuel quickly. If the iron was this hot, the fire had been stoked recently. Vance wasn't out on a multi-day hunting trip. He was close. He could be walking back across the clearing at this very second. The timeline had just collapsed.

Alex moved faster, his gun leading the way down a narrow, pitch-black hallway at the back of the bunker. There were two doors at the very end. The door on the left was standard wood, hanging slightly open, revealing a filthy, unmade mattress. Vance's room.

The door on the right was solid, reinforced steel. There was no doorknob. Instead, a thick, heavy-duty industrial padlock was bolted to a thick exterior hasp, securing the door flush against the metal frame. It was the exact lock mechanism Chloe had drawn in her sketchbook. Alex stared at it. He was standing right outside the cage.

Alex ran his flashlight over the solid steel door and the thick padlock. His eyes caught the edges of the doorframe. The wood surrounding the reinforced steel was completely different from the rotting, water-damaged timber of the rest of the bunker. It was newer. Vance hadn't kept Chloe in a padlock vault. This cage was built after Chloe escaped. Vance was so consumed by the girl who climbed out the window that he locked his remaining captive in a steel box to guarantee she could never do the same.

He holstered his gun and reached into his coat, pulling out a hardened steel pry bar. He didn't have time for the bolt cutters, and the padlock was too thick for them anyway. He wedged the flattened edge of the bar deep behind the metal hasp, bracing his boots against the bottom of the steel door. He took a deep breath, thinking of the tiny, yellowed infant's sock sitting in Chloe's limp hand in the ICU.

Alex pulled back with devastating force. The veins in his neck bulged as he threw the entirety of his two-hundred-and-twenty-pound frame against the lever. The wood surrounding the metal frame began to splinter and shriek. *Crack!* The thick screws tore out of the wall frame. The hasp gave way, and the solid steel door violently swung outward.

Alex dropped the pry bar. He pulled his tactical flashlight from his pocket and clicked it on, sweeping the blinding beam of white light into the pitch-black room. The beam cut through the dust, hitting the far concrete wall.

Huddled in the deepest corner of the room, curled into a defensive, trembling ball, was a girl. She was wearing a ragged, oversized grey sweater that hung off her emaciated frame. Her dark, matted hair shielded her face as she threw her hands up, letting out a sharp, terrified whimper against the sudden, blinding light. It was Tyra. She was fourteen years old, and she was entirely consumed by the dark.

Tyra scrambled backward, her shoulders scraping against the concrete as she tried to fuse herself with the wall. Her chest heaved with frantic, ragged breaths. She expected the monster. She expected violence.

Alex immediately clicked the flashlight off, plunging the room into a softer, ambient dimness. He didn't step toward her. He knew his imposing size was terrifying. Instead, Alex dropped slowly to one knee, making himself as small as physically possible. He kept his hands completely visible, resting them gently on his thighs.

"Tyra," Alex said. His voice was a low, steady, and incredibly gentle rumble. It was the exact same voice he used to pull his wife out of her night terrors. "My name is Alex."

The girl didn't move. She was trembling so violently her teeth were chattering.

"I'm not going to hurt you," Alex promised, his heart breaking as he looked at the feral terror in her eyes. He took a slow breath. "Chloe sent me."

At the sound of the name, Tyra completely froze. The frantic, terrified whimpering stopped. Slowly, hesitantly, she lowered her trembling hands from her face, peering through her tangled hair.

Alex extended one large, steady hand across the dark space between them, palm up.

"She sent me to bring you home," Alex whispered. "Are you ready to leave the dark?"

23 THE EXTRACTION

ALEX

Alex knelt on the cold concrete. The solid steel door of the cage hung open behind him, casting a dim, ambient wedge of light into the pitch-black room. He didn't move a muscle. In the deepest corner of the cell, Tyra was pressed so hard against the wall she looked as though she were trying to fuse with the concrete. She had her knees pulled tightly to her chest, her thin arms wrapped around her shins. She was trembling violently, her dark, matted hair shielding her face. She wasn't looking at a rescuer. She was looking at a towering, two-hundred-and-twenty-pound man dressed in black tactical gear, blocking the only exit. She was looking at another monster.

"Tyra," Alex repeated softly. His voice was a low, steady rumble. "I'm not going to hurt you."

Tyra flinched. She didn't look up, but her voice scratched against the silence of the room—a raspy, broken whisper from a throat that rarely used words. "My dad says the girl who left was a liar," she whispered, her body rocking slightly. "My dad says everyone lies."

The word hit Alex like a physical blow to the chest. *Dad.* The blood froze in his veins. He looked at the hollowed-out, terrified fourteen-year-old girl in the dirt, and the frantic, jagged words from Chloe's journal suddenly clicked into a devastating reality. He wasn't just rescuing a captive. He was looking at his wife's daughter.

Alex felt a crushing, sickening weight settle in his chest. Arthur Vance hadn't just kept her locked in a box; he had poisoned her mind with the ghost of the girl who had escaped. Tyra didn't remember Chloe as a mother or a sister.

She only knew the story of the teenager who had abandoned her to the dark. Alex knew that his size and his weapons were useless here. Reason wouldn't work, and force would shatter her completely. If he wanted to save her, he had to give her the one thing Arthur Vance had stolen from her for fourteen years: agency.

Alex reached down to his waist. He unclipped the thick tactical belt holding his handgun. He slid the entire rig across the filthy concrete floor, pushing it completely out of his own reach. Tyra's breath hitched, her eyes darting through her hair to track the weapon as it slid away. Alex slowly pulled off his thick winter gloves, tossing them aside to expose his bare, human hands. Then, he shifted his weight off his knee and sat flat on the freezing floor. He made himself lower than her.

"He's right," Alex said. He didn't use a placating, childish tone. He spoke to her with absolute, devastating honesty. "She did leave you behind."

Tyra froze, the rocking motion stopping instantly.

"She was sixteen years old, and she was terrified," Alex continued, his voice thick with the grief he carried for his wife. "She climbed out a window to save herself. And she has been drowning in the guilt of it ever since. It broke her mind, Tyra. But she never forgot you."

Tyra slowly lifted her head. Her light brown face was smeared with dirt, and hollowed out by malnutrition. But beneath the grime, Alex saw the striking, unmistakable echo of Chloe's dark eyes. Alex reached for the zipper of his insulated winter parka. He pulled it down, slipped his broad shoulders out of the sleeves, and bunched the thick black coat in his hands. He pushed it gently across the concrete until it rested a few feet away from her battered sneakers. He stood up slowly. He left the coat and his weapon on the ground.

"I am not going to drag you out of here," Alex said, looking down at her. "I am going to leave this steel door wide open. If you are ready to leave the dark, put the coat on and follow me."

Alex did the most terrifying thing a man could do in a hostile environment. He turned his back on her. He walked out of the cage and stepped into the dim hallway. He didn't look back. He stood in the silence of the rotting bunker, his heart hammering against his ribs in the freezing air. Ten seconds passed. Then twenty. The silence was agonizing.

Then, he heard the soft, hesitant rustle of nylon. A moment later, Tyra stepped out of the steel doorway. She was entirely swallowed by his oversized black parka, the hem dragging against the floorboards. She was clutching the thick fabric tightly around her chest like a suit of armor. She looked up at him, her eyes wide with a fragile, desperate trust. She had made the choice.

Alex let out a slow, shaking breath. He knelt down, retrieved his gun belt from the floor of the cage, and strapped it back on, keeping the weapon securely holstered. "Stay close," he whispered.

He guided her down the hallway. Tyra's movements were painfully slow. Her muscles were stiff, unaccustomed to walking more than a few paces at a time. When they reached the front door of the bunker, Alex pushed it wide open. The freezing winter wind howled into the room. Tyra gasped, throwing her arm up to shield her eyes. The sheer, expansive void of the pale grey sky and the towering pine trees was a terrifying sensory shock after a lifetime in a sensory-deprived box.

"I've got you," Alex promised, resting a gentle hand on her shoulder. "Just to the tree line."

They stepped out of the bunker and onto the frozen dirt clearing. They were exposed. They made it twenty yards. They were halfway to the severed perimeter fence when the ground beneath their boots began to vibrate. Alex stopped. He turned his head toward the dense trees bordering the logging road.

The deep, mechanical rumble of a roaring diesel engine echoed through the silent forest. A second later, the twin beams of a truck's headlights swept violently across the snow, illuminating the rusted wire of the fence. Arthur Vance was back.

The truck was less than a quarter mile down the access road, and it was moving fast. Alex's analytical mind immediately ran the brutal variables. The deep snow meant Tyra couldn't run. If they tried to make a dash for the open gate to reach his hidden SUV, the headlights would catch them in the clearing. Vance would run them down with the truck, or he would simply shoot them in the back. The path to the vehicle was dead. They couldn't outrun him. They had to hide.

"Hold on to me," Alex ordered. He didn't wait for her to process the panic. Alex scooped Tyra up into his arms, ignoring the burning cold biting through his thin sweater. He abandoned the path leading to the SUV and sprinted in the exact opposite direction. He carried her past the bunker, plunging directly into the dense, unbroken pine forest at the rear of the property. He moved with desperate, calculated precision, intentionally stepping hard into the snow drifts and brushing past the low-hanging branches to break their tracks before the truck pulled into the clearing.

The headlights flared against the front of the bunker just as Alex and Tyra were swallowed by the shadows of the Michigamee woods. The trap had closed.

CHLOE

I am backed against the wall of the kitchenette. The smell of scorched grease is so thick I can taste it on my tongue. The peeling yellow linoleum floor feels sticky beneath my bare feet.

The phantom in the corner is laughing at me, his face blurred in the shadows, telling me I belong here. He tells me I am exactly where I deserve to be because I left them both behind. Tyra in the dark. Isabella in the blood.

I press my hands over my ears, squeezing my eyes shut, waiting for the dense, suffocating heat of the rotting house to finally crush me. But it doesn't.

Something shifts. The smell of the grease suddenly thins, replaced by the sharp, clean scent of pine needles. The oppressive heat of the room fractures. I shiver.

A phantom winter wind is blowing through the kitchenette, cutting through the hallucination like a razor blade. I open my eyes.

The locked front door of my mind—the door I have kept deadbolted for fourteen years—is rattling. Someone is out there in the freezing dark. And they are trying to break the lock.

24 THE MICHIGAMEE HUNT

ALEX

The Michigamee forest was a sprawling, frozen ocean of absolute darkness. Alex and Tyra were buried deep beneath the low-hanging branches of a towering evergreen, half-swallowed by a deep snow drift. The silence of the woods was deafening, broken only by the violent, ragged sound of their own breathing. The cold was catastrophic.

Without his thick winter parka, the sub-zero wind cut straight through Alex's thin sweater like a serrated blade. He couldn't feel his fingers. His tactical boots felt like blocks of ice, and violent, uncontrollable shivers were already wracking his chest. His mind, usually so structured and controlled, stripped away every thought except pure, primal survival. He knew exactly what his body was doing. He was rapidly losing core heat, and hypothermia would kill him in less than an hour.

Beside him, Tyra was curled into a tight ball, completely swallowed by his black coat. She was clutching the thick nylon so tightly her knuckles were white, her eyes wide and fixed blindly on the dark trees ahead of them. *Clang.* The sharp, metallic shriek of the bunker's steel door being thrown open violently echoed through the silent woods. Tyra flinched so hard she hit her head against the trunk of the pine tree. She let out a soft, terrified whimper, pressing both hands over her mouth to stifle the sound.

A few seconds later, a brilliant, piercing beam of white light sliced through the trees. It swept across the frozen clearing and hit the edge of the tree line. Arthur Vance wasn't just looking; he was hunting. The high-powered beam swept back and forth, cutting through the shadows, slowly and methodically tracking the deep footprints Alex had left in the fresh snow. Alex watched the beam of light inch closer.

He looked at the terrifying reality of their situation. Vance knew these woods blindly. He was dressed for the lethal weather, and he was armed with a hunting rifle. Alex and Tyra could not outrun him in knee-deep snow, and they could not wait him out because the freezing temperatures would stop their hearts before sunrise. Evasion was a death sentence. If Alex stayed hidden beneath these branches with Tyra, they were both going to die in the snow.

The only way to guarantee her survival was to change the dynamic of the hunt. He had to stop hiding. He had to become the bait. Alex turned his head slowly. He reached out with a numb, shaking hand and gently gripped Tyra's shoulder. She looked at him, her dark eyes completely consumed by terror as the flashlight beam cut through the trees just fifty yards to their left.

"Listen to me," Alex whispered, his voice a strained, icy rasp. He held her gaze with absolute, unwavering intensity. "I am going to step out. I am going to draw him away from you."

Tyra shook her head frantically, her hands gripping his wrist, pleading with him silently.

"You have to be brave for just a few more minutes," Alex commanded softly. "When you hear the gunshot, you do not scream. You do not look back. You stand up, and you run straight south. Keep the North Star at your back, and do not stop running until your boots hit the dirt logging road. Someone will be there. Do you understand?"

Tyra's chest heaved. A single tear escaped her eye, instantly freezing on her dirt-streaked cheek. Slowly, she gave a single, trembling nod.

CHLOE

I am trapped in the corner of the rotting kitchenette. The monster in the shadows is laughing at me, his voice a low, brutal scrape against my skull. He tells me I belong in the dark.

He tells me I am exactly where I deserve to be. I press my hands over my ears, waiting for the suffocating heat of the grease and the damp wood to finally crush me. But something is wrong.

For days, there has been a warm, comforting tether anchoring my right hand. A lifeline pulling me back from the absolute dark, keeping me from slipping entirely away. But suddenly, the warmth is gone.

My hand feels empty. Cold. No, not empty. My fingers curl inward instinctively. I feel something small resting in my palm.

Soft, worn cotton. The faint, undeniable texture of a tiny woven sock. The smell of scorched grease falters. The rotting yellow linoleum beneath my bare feet feels less permanent.

The phantom Artie steps forward, his calloused hands reaching for my throat. He expects me to cower. He expects me to squeeze my eyes shut and wait for the man with the thudding footsteps to come and lock the doors.

He expects me to be the terrified sixteen-year-old girl who climbs out the window. But the tether is gone. The warm hand is gone.

No one is coming to stand between me and the dark. If I want to survive, if I ever want to hold that tiny piece of cotton in the light again, I cannot wait to be rescued. I have to be the one to kill the monster.

The suffocating, crushing weight of fourteen years of guilt suddenly shatters. I drop my hands from my ears. I stop crying.

I look up at the phantom reaching for me. I stand up, plant my feet firmly on the rotting floorboards, and clench my hands into brutal, violent fists.

ALEX

The flashlight beam swept across the snow, illuminating the trunk of an oak tree just thirty yards away. Alex forced himself up. His legs were numb, his joints screaming in protest against the lethal cold. He drew the large-caliber handgun from his hip, the freezing steel burning against his bare palm. He gripped it with both hands. He looked down at Tyra one last time. He gave her a single, silent nod.

Alex stepped out from the cover of the evergreen. He stood at his full, imposing height in the deep snow. He didn't try to sneak. He raised his rugged boot and intentionally brought it down hard on a thick, dead pine branch buried in the drift.

Crack! The sound was as loud as a firecracker. The flashlight beam violently whipped through the dark trees. It swept past the evergreens, cut through the falling snow, and locked dead center onto Alex's chest, blinding him instantly. From the absolute darkness behind the piercing light, the cold, metallic clack of a hunting rifle chambering a round echoed through the Michigamee woods.

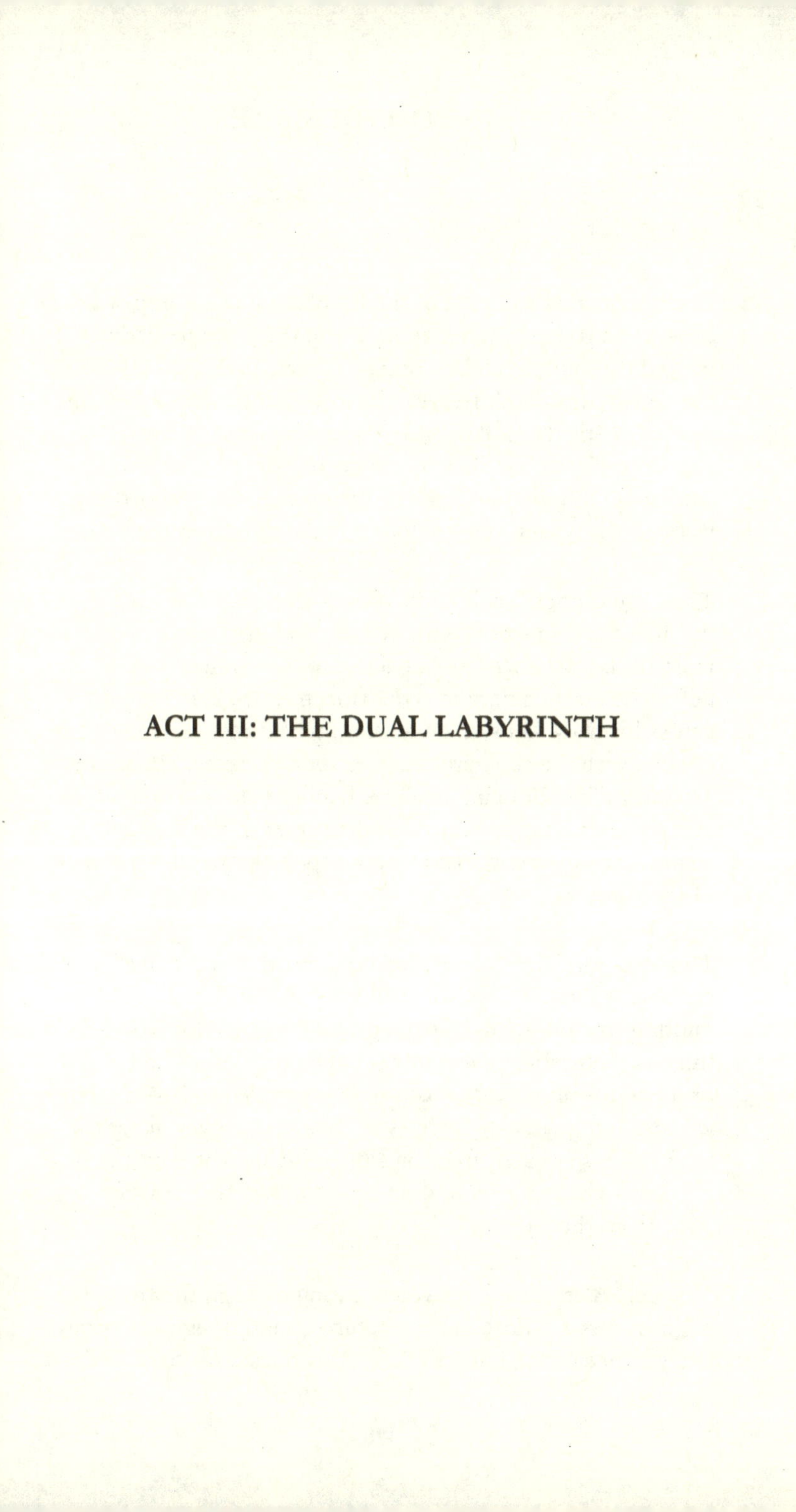

ACT III: THE DUAL LABYRINTH

25 **INTO THE MAZE**

ALEX

The blinding white beam of the flashlight locked onto Alex's chest for a fraction of a second. From the absolute darkness behind the light, a brilliant orange muzzle flash tore through the night. Alex didn't freeze. The instant the light hit him, his survival instincts took over. He threw his solid frame sideways, diving blindly into the deep snow drift just as the deafening, thunderous crack of the hunting rifle echoed through the Michigamee woods. He didn't outrun the bullet.

The large caliber round clipped his left shoulder, tearing through the thin wool of his sweater and ripping the meat from his collarbone. The impact spun him violently in the air before he crashed hard into the frozen earth. Pain erupted across his chest—a sudden, blistering heat that violently clashed with the sub-zero air. Alex didn't scream. He hit the ground rolling, bringing his large handgun up. He fired twice into the dark, aiming directly at the center of the flashlight beam. The deafening roar of his weapon shattered the silence of the forest.

The beam of light violently jerked upward into the tree canopy. A second later, the distinct, metallic clatter of the hunting rifle hitting the frozen ground echoed through the trees as the flashlight abruptly snapped off. Vance had dropped his primary weapon. Alex scrambled to his feet. His left arm hung uselessly at his side, blood already soaking the sleeve of his sweater, freezing almost the instant it hit the air. He didn't check the wound. He had to draw the monster away from the girl.

"Vance!" Alex roared, his voice tearing through the freezing night. It was a primal, gut-wrenching sound designed to draw every ounce of the hunter's rage. Alex turned his back to the south and broke into a dead, desperate sprint directly east, plunging deeper into the unforgiving, pitch-black labyrinth of the evergreens.

TYRA

The thunder of the gunshot hit Tyra like a physical blow. She flinched so violently she bit her own lip, the sharp taste of copper flooding her mouth. Her hands flew up to cover her ears, and her eyes squeezed shut. She waited for the thudding footsteps. She waited for the hands to drag her back into the dark. *Do not scream. Do not look back.* The imposing man's voice echoed in her mind. It was the first time in fourteen years someone had given her a command that wasn't designed to hurt her.

Another string of deafening shots rang out, followed by a raw, furious shout echoing through the trees, moving further away. Tyra opened her eyes. The woods immediately surrounding her were empty and terrifyingly silent. She scrambled out of the snowbank. The oversized black parka dragged against the ice, swallowing her emaciated frame. For the first time in her life, there were no concrete walls. There was no rusted steel ceiling. The sheer, infinite expanse of the dark woods and the towering trees felt like a different kind of cage—one that was too big, too loud, and entirely unprotected. She turned her back to the distant sound of the gunfire. She waded into the knee-deep snow, dragging the rugged boots she had stolen from the bunker, and began to run.

ALEX

Alex pushed violently through a dense thicket of dead brush. The thorns tore at his face and his bare hands, but the freezing wind had completely numbed his skin. His lungs burned. Every breath felt like inhaling broken glass. The adrenaline that had carried him through the first half mile was beginning to crash, replaced by a crushing, terrifying exhaustion. He slowed his pace, leaning heavily against the trunk of an ancient oak tree to catch his breath.

He looked down at the pristine white snow at his boots. His heart sank. A stark, undeniable trail of dark red droplets painted the snow directly behind him. The wound on his shoulder was bleeding heavily. In this pristine environment, he wasn't just leaving footprints; he was leaving a literal roadmap for a seasoned tracker. He couldn't just run in a straight line. If he did, Vance would catch him before he covered another mile.

Alex forced himself off the tree. He had to turn these woods into a maze. He began to intentionally loop his tracks, wading through the thickest, most impenetrable patches of briars he could find to mask the blood. He doubled back on his own footprints, breaking branches and disturbing the snow in the wrong directions, doing everything in his power to slow the monster down. Every extra minute he bought was another mile Tyra could put between herself and the cage.

TYRA

Tyra’s foot caught on a thick, buried pine root. She pitched forward, crying out as she hit the ground hard. The heavy snow rushed into the collar of the oversized parka, freezing against her neck and her cheeks. She lay there in the dark, her chest heaving, her weak muscles completely failing her. The cold was unbearable. The silence was suffocating.

The darkest, most broken part of her mind whispered a terrifying thought. The cage was warm. The cage was the only world she knew. Out here, the dark was endless. If she just stopped moving, if she just closed her eyes and let the freezing snow cover her, she wouldn't have to be afraid anymore. She curled her knees toward her chest.

As she shifted, the insulated nylon of the black coat brushed against her chin. It still smelled faintly of the brave man who had bled for her. He had taken off his armor and handed it to a stranger. He had stepped into the line of fire so she could live. Tyra opened her eyes. Directly above her, the thick canopy of the pine trees swayed in the bitter wind. The heavy winter clouds parted, just for a moment, revealing a single, piercing point of light in the bruised purple sky.

The North Star. *Keep it at your back*, he had said. Tyra gritted her teeth. She planted her freezing hands in the snow and forced herself to her feet. She pulled the thick coat tightly around her shoulders, turned her back to the pale starlight, and kept walking south.

26 THE HALLWAY OF DOORS

CHLOE

The phantom Artie has retreated into the shadows of the rotting kitchenette. He knows I am awake now. He knows the fear isn't paralyzing me anymore.

I don't wait for him to come back. I walk toward the peeling, grease-stained door leading out of the kitchen. I reach out, grab the rusted brass handle, and pull it open.

I don't step out into the frozen dirt clearing of Michigamee County. I step into a long, impossible hallway. The walls are stretched and distorted, fading into absolute pitch-blackness in both directions.

Lining the walls are dozens of solid wooden doors. This is the architecture of my own trauma. These are the memories I locked away, the boxes I shoved deep into the basement of my mind so I could pretend to be a normal wife living a normal life.

The phantom is hiding behind one of them. He is using my worst nightmares as a shield. I don't cower.

I don't turn around. I step out of the kitchenette, the rotting door slamming shut behind me, and I walk straight into the labyrinth.

ALEX

Alex collapsed against the rough bark of a pine tree, his chest heaving violently. The numbness was spreading. The blistering heat of the gunshot wound had faded into a deep, sickening ache that radiated down his entire left side. His arm was completely useless, hanging dead at his side. He looked down. The dark blood was still flowing freely, soaking through the wool of his sweater and dripping onto the pristine snow. If he didn't stop the bleeding, the cold wouldn't be what killed him.

Alex bit down hard on his bottom lip. Using his teeth and his one good hand, he gripped the hem of his torn sweater and ripped a long, thick strip of the wool free. He wrapped the makeshift tourniquet tightly around his shoulder, pulling it with his teeth until the fabric dug brutally into his torn flesh. He squeezed his eyes shut to fight off the wave of nausea as the bleeding finally slowed to a sluggish crawl.

Then, he heard it. *Crunch. Crunch.* It was faint, but in the absolute silence of the Michigamee woods, it sounded like a hammer hitting an anvil. The slow, methodical, thudding footsteps of a man who knew exactly where he was going. Arthur Vance wasn't running. He wasn't rushing blindly through the brush. He was pacing himself, tracking the blood drops in the snow like a seasoned predator casually wearing down wounded prey.

Running was no longer an option. If Alex kept moving, he would just bleed out and collapse from exhaustion, leaving his back totally exposed. He had to stop. He had to set a trap. Alex pushed off the tree, his boots dragging heavily in the snow. He scanned the dark woods ahead, looking for an advantage.

CHLOE

I walk down the dark hallway. The floorboards creak beneath my bare feet. A few yards ahead, a sliver of soft, warm light bleeds out from beneath one of the heavy doors.

It doesn't smell like scorched grease or damp earth. It smells like fresh paint. It smells like lavender and baby powder.

I stop. My throat tightens. I know exactly what is behind this door.

I push it open. The room is bathed in golden light. The walls are painted a soft, perfect yellow.

In the center of the room sits the white wooden crib. Isabella's nursery. A low, scraping laugh echoes from the shadowy corner behind the rocking chair.

The phantom Artie's voice slithers into my ears, twisting the knife directly into my chest. "You failed her," the phantom whispers. "You let her bleed out. You built this beautiful room, and then you broke her. You belong in the dark with me."

Tears blur my vision. The urge to fall to my knees and surrender to the crushing, suffocating weight of the grief is almost overpowering. It is a trap.

He wants me to drown in it. I take a shaking breath. I walk slowly across the thick carpet.

I look down into the empty white crib, staring at the perfectly folded pink blankets. I let the tears fall, but I don't break. "I did lose her," I whisper to the empty room. "And it tore my soul in half."

I turn around, facing the dark corner where the phantom's voice is hiding. I clench my hands into fists. "But the grief is mine," I say, my voice growing louder, sharper. "The love is mine. It is not yours to use."

The golden light violently flickers. The nursery walls shatter like brittle glass, exploding outward into a million pieces of blinding white light, leaving me standing back in the dark hallway. The phantom is running out of places to hide. I keep moving forward.

TYRA

Tyra's legs were shaking so violently she could barely keep her balance. Every step through the deep, heavy snowdrifts felt like wading through wet cement. The oversized boots she had taken from the bunker were rubbing her bare heels raw, leaving blisters that had already popped and frozen against the leather. Her lungs burned. Her vision was starting to tunnel. The overwhelming urge to just lie down in the snow and sleep was fighting the desperate, primal command to keep the North Star at her back.

She paused, leaning heavily against a snow-covered boulder, gasping for air. Then, the absolute, dead silence of the woods was broken. It wasn't the wind. It wasn't the terrifying crack of a rifle. It was a low, steady, unnatural hum.

Tyra turned her head, straining her ears. The sound was faint, drifting through the dense pines from somewhere straight ahead. It was the loud, rhythmic grind of rubber tires rolling over an icy surface. A road.

Hope, terrifying and fragile, flared in her chest. She pushed off the rock, ignoring the agonizing pain in her feet, and forced herself to walk faster toward the sound.

ALEX

Alex found the choke point. Two ancient pine trees had been uprooted in a storm years ago, falling across each other to form a tight, V-shaped funnel of dead wood and thick, impenetrable brush. There was only one way through it. Alex wedged his broad frame deep into the shadows of the fallen trunks, burying himself in the snow and the dead pine needles.

He rested his right forearm against a thick branch to steady his shaking hand. He leveled the large-caliber handgun directly at the narrow gap between the trees. He slowed his breathing, forcing his chest to rise and fall in shallow, silent increments. He waited.

The crunch of the boots grew louder. A looming shadow detached from the dark tree line fifty feet away. Arthur Vance stepped into the clearing leading up to the fallen pines. He wasn't holding his rifle. He was staring at the dark red drops of blood leading directly into the V-shaped gap. Vance didn't look up. He stepped right into the center of the choke point.

Alex exhaled a plume of white breath into the freezing air. He tightened his freezing finger on the trigger.

27 THE CHOKE POINT

ALEX

Alex exhaled a plume of white breath into the freezing air, his right hand perfectly steady in the darkness of the brush. He tightened his numb finger on the trigger. The large-caliber handgun roared, spitting a blinding tongue of orange fire into the dark choke point.

But Arthur Vance had the feral, hyper-tuned instincts of a man who had survived in the wild for fourteen years. He didn't freeze. A microsecond before the hammer struck, he saw the faint glint of the barrel buried in the pine needles. Vance twisted violently to the right. The bullet didn't hit center mass. It tore through the stiff nylon of Vance's coat, grazing his ribs in a spray of dark blood.

Vance didn't retreat. He didn't even stumble. He let out a raw, guttural scream of absolute rage. He dropped the long hunting rifle into the snow, reached to his belt, and drew a brutal, serrated hunting knife. Before Alex could fire a second shot, Vance charged directly into the brush. The impact was devastating. Vance slammed into Alex's chest, driving the air from his lungs and sending the large handgun flying into the deep snow. The two men crashed backward, breaking through the dead branches of the fallen pines.

The fight was ugly, visceral, and desperate. Alex was formidable, but he was operating with one useless, bleeding arm, his limbs sluggish from the catastrophic cold. Vance was relentless, driven by pure, violent fury. Vance drove his knee into Alex's torn shoulder. White-hot agony exploded behind Alex's eyes, blinding him for a fraction of a second. Vance raised the brutal knife, aiming straight for Alex's throat.

Alex roared, ignoring the blinding pain. He drove his right fist upward with everything he had left. His knuckles connected squarely with Vance's face. The sickening crunch of shattering bone echoed in the narrow gap. Vance's head snapped back, his nose flattened and pouring blood over his beard. But Vance didn't fall. Staggering backward, blinded by his own blood, he kicked out blindly. The rugged toe of his winter boot connected with the center of Alex's chest.

Alex was already off-balance, the ground beneath his boots giving way to a steep, hidden incline. He fell backward into the dark. The snowbank collapsed beneath his weight. Alex tumbled violently down the steep face of a hidden ravine, his body slamming against jagged rocks and buried tree roots. He fell for what felt like an eternity, completely out of control, until he slammed hard into the frozen earth at the bottom of the gorge.

The breath left him in a ragged, bloody gasp. He lay in the pitch-black snow, entirely paralyzed by the impact. High above him, at the edge of the broken ravine, Vance stood silhouetted against the dark sky. He spat a mouthful of blood into the snow, stared down into the black abyss for a long moment, and turned away. He assumed the fall or the freezing cold would finish the job. He had a daughter to catch.

CHLOE

I walk further down the impossible, pitch-black hallway of my own mind. I don't hesitate. I reach for the solid brass knob of the next door and push it open.

The freezing wind hits me immediately, howling through a torn window screen. I am standing in my childhood bedroom inside the Michigamee compound. The walls are bare, rotting wood.

The floor is covered in a thin layer of dust. The phantom Artie is standing by the open window. He is looking out into the dark, but he isn't alone.

Cradled in his broad, shadowy arms is an infant. Tyra. She is crying, a thin, terrified wail that cuts straight through the wind and into the deepest, most broken part of my soul.

The phantom turns his face toward me. His eyes are hollow and cruel. "This is the moment you became a monster," he whispers, his voice scraping against the walls.

"You left a daughter with her father. You knew exactly the kind of man I was. You knew exactly what I would do to her in the dark. And you climbed out the window anyway."

He holds the crying infant out over the dark sill. He is trying to force me to relive the darkest sin of my life. He is waiting for me to break.

He is waiting for me to beg for a forgiveness I know he will never give me. I look at the open window. I look at the crying baby.

My chest heaves, but I don't drop to my knees. "I was sixteen years old," I say. My voice is shaking, but it is loud enough to cut through the howling wind.

"I was a child." The phantom freezes. "I didn't leave her because I was a monster," I say, stepping closer, my bare feet firm on the rotting wood.

"I left because I was terrified. I left because if I stayed, you would have destroyed us both. I did the only thing I could do to survive."

I stop apologizing to the darkness. I look at the open window, and for the first time in fourteen years, I forgive the terrified teenage girl who climbed out of it.

The phantom Artie lets out a deafening, agonizing roar. His greatest weapon isn't my fear—it is my guilt. And I just took it away from him.

The memory of the bedroom violently shatters. The walls splinter, the floor drops away, and the phantom explodes into a cloud of screaming black ash, fleeing deeper into the labyrinth of my mind.

TYRA

Tyra threw her weight against a dense wall of frozen pine branches, tearing her way through the final barrier of the Michigamee woods. She stumbled forward and fell to her knees. Her torn, bleeding hands didn't hit snow or dirt. They hit solid, icy asphalt. She had reached the edge of the map. She had found the logging road.

She knelt on the freezing pavement, gasping for air, her head hanging low. Suddenly, a brilliant, blinding pair of twin headlights flared to life just twenty feet to her left. Tyra violently flinched, throwing her arms over her face and scrambling backward on the ice. She expected the battered, roaring diesel truck of the monster. But the engine was a soft, quiet purr.

It was a sleek, black luxury sedan, idling completely out of place on the shoulder of the desolate wilderness road. The driver's side door flew open. A man stepped out into the freezing wind. He was wearing an expensive, tailored wool overcoat. He was shaking uncontrollably, his eyes wide with absolute terror as he stared into the dark woods. He was looking for a mountain of a man in tactical gear. He was looking for Alex.

Instead, he saw a fourteen-year-old girl, completely swallowed by a ruined black parka, collapsed on the ice in front of his headlights. Jason froze. Fourteen years ago, he had stood in an alleyway and chosen to hide a traumatized girl because he was afraid of the monster in the woods. He had lived every day since as a coward.

Jason looked at Tyra. He heard the faint, distant echo of gunfire from deep inside the trees. This time, Jason didn't turn away. He broke into a run, his expensive leather shoes slipping on the ice. He dropped to his knees right beside her, wrapping his trembling arms around her shaking shoulders. "I've got you," Jason gasped, his voice breaking as he pulled her to her feet, shielding her from the wind. "I've got you. Let's go."

28 **THE ASCENT**

JASON

Jason practically tore the solid passenger door of the sedan open. The freezing wind howled across the icy asphalt, but he didn't feel it. His heart was hammering a frantic, terrifying rhythm against his ribs. He grabbed the emaciated, trembling girl by the shoulders of the oversized black parka and shoved her gently but forcefully into the leather passenger seat. He slammed the door shut, sprinting around the hood of the car, his expensive dress shoes slipping dangerously on the black ice.

He threw himself behind the wheel. His hands were shaking so violently he could barely grip the gearshift. He slammed the car into drive and looked up at the rearview mirror. Deep in the tree line, a looming shadow was moving through the snow. Arthur Vance was coming. Jason didn't breathe. He slammed his foot down on the gas pedal. The luxury sedan fishtailed, the rear tires spinning wildly, screaming against the ice before finally catching traction. The car launched forward, tearing away from the edge of the map, leaving the dark, suffocating Michigamee woods behind.

ALEX

The cold was no longer just a temperature. It was a physical weight crushing his chest. Alex opened his eyes. The absolute, pitch-black darkness of the ravine swam in and out of focus. He was lying flat on his back in a bed of jagged, snow-covered rocks. Every breath was a jagged knife twisting in his lungs. At least two of his ribs were cracked from the fall. His left shoulder was completely numb, the makeshift wool tourniquet frozen solid against the torn flesh. He lay there for a long, agonizing moment, staring up at the narrow sliver of pale starlight visible through the canopy fifty feet above him.

The woods were completely silent. Vance hadn't climbed down to finish the job. Through the ringing in his ears, Alex realized why. The faint, distant squeal of tires spinning on ice echoed through the cold air. An engine. Alex's breath caught in his throat. He had hidden his SUV a mile away. Tyra didn't know how to drive, let alone navigate a large vehicle on black ice. Someone else was out there on the logging road, and they were tearing away from the compound.

A surge of raw, primal adrenaline cut through the agonizing pain. Vance wasn't climbing down into the ravine because Vance was heading back to the clearing. If the monster got behind the wheel of that battered diesel truck, he would hunt that fleeing car down on the treacherous, winding county roads and run it straight off a cliff. Alex didn't know who was behind the wheel, but he knew he couldn't let Vance follow them. The mission wasn't over.

Alex forced himself onto his right side. He dug his good hand into the snow, blindly searching the frozen earth until his fingers brushed against cold steel. He gripped the large-caliber handgun and shoved it deep into his belt.

CHLOE

I reach the very end of the long, impossible hallway in my mind. There are no more wooden doors. The floor ends at a broad, solid iron threshold.

It is completely silent. I reach out and push the iron door open. There is no memory behind it.

There is no rotting kitchenette, no golden nursery, no open window with the freezing wind. It is a completely blank, infinite white void.

The phantom Artie is backed into the absolute corner of the empty room. He is entirely stripped of his shadows. He has no guilt to weaponize. He has no illusions to hide behind.

In the stark, blinding white light, he isn't a towering, terrifying monster anymore. He is just a man. A pathetic, cruel remnant of a nightmare that I have finally outgrown.

I don't yell. I don't raise my fists. I walk across the white floor, stopping inches away from him.

I look directly into his hollow, desperate eyes. "You don't exist in my world anymore," I say. My voice is quiet, steady, and absolutely final.

The phantom opens his mouth to speak, but no sound comes out. In the brilliant white light, his form begins to dissolve, flaking away like dry ash in the wind, until there is absolutely nothing left.

I am completely alone in the light. I close my eyes. I take a deep, clear breath. And I prepare to wake up.

ALEX

Alex stood at the absolute bottom of the icy gorge. He looked up at the sheer, vertical wall of snow, jagged rock, and exposed roots. It was a fifty-foot climb straight up. He reached out with his right hand and dug his freezing fingers into a deep crevice in the stone. He pulled his solid frame upward, his boots scraping frantically against the ice for purchase.

The ascent was brutal. Every inch was a violent, agonizing war against gravity and his own failing body. The cracked ribs ground together with every pull. The useless, bleeding left arm dragged against the rocks. The cold ripped the breath from his throat. But he didn't stop. He visualized the rusted metal truck. He visualized the icy roads. He drove his right fist into the frozen earth, finding a thick, buried pine root. He hauled himself upward with a final, desperate roar of exertion.

Alex dragged his battered, bleeding body over the snowy ledge. He collapsed onto the flat ground, gasping for air. But he didn't stay down. He forced himself to his knees, looking through the dense, dark trees toward the center of the compound. A quarter mile away, the blinding headlights of the battered diesel truck snapped on, illuminating the dirt clearing. The roaring engine came to life. Vance was leaving.

Alex didn't hide. He didn't seek cover. He drew the large-caliber handgun from his belt, forced himself to his feet, and broke into a dead sprint straight toward the blinding light.

29 **THE INTERCEPTION**

ALEX

Alex dragged his battered body out of the tree line. Fifty yards away, the dirt clearing of the compound was bathed in the harsh, blinding glare of twin headlights. The battered diesel truck sat idling in front of the rusted bunker, dark exhaust pouring from the tailpipe into the freezing night sky. Arthur Vance was behind the wheel. The gears ground together with a violent, metallic shriek as Vance forcefully slammed the transmission into drive. The truck lurched forward, the rugged studded tires tearing into the frozen earth.

Alex watched from the shadows, his breathing shallow and ragged. Through the glare of the lights, he could see Vance's silhouette in the cab. The man wasn't moving with the cold, methodical precision he had shown in the woods. He was frantic. He was slamming his fists against the steering wheel, his head whipping back and forth. The terrifying reality suddenly clicked in Alex's mind. Vance wasn't just chasing an escaped prisoner. Tyra was an infant when Chloe climbed out that window fourteen years ago. She had been raised in that padlock cage by one man. Tyra wasn't property to Arthur Vance. She was his blood. She was his daughter.

A monster hunting for sport was dangerous. A monster terrified of losing his child was completely unhinged. If Vance made it to the logging road, he wouldn't just run that fleeing car off the ice—he would tear the metal apart with his hands to get his daughter back. Alex didn't know who was driving, but he knew they wouldn't survive a collision with this machine. Alex couldn't outrun the truck, and with a freezing, shaking hand, he couldn't guarantee a kill shot through the thick glass of the windshield. To save Tyra, he had to kill the vehicle itself.

Alex stepped entirely out of the shadows. He didn't run for the perimeter fence. He walked directly into the center of the frozen clearing, placing his broken, bleeding body dead in the path of the accelerating three-ton machine.

CHLOE

The infinite white void of my mind suddenly, violently fractures. It shatters like a pane of glass hit by a hammer.

The absolute silence is ripped away, replaced by a deafening, rhythmic shrieking. My eyes snap open.

The transition is brutal. Blinding, harsh fluorescent light burns my retinas, forcing me to blink rapidly against the agonizing sting. The suffocating smell of damp wood and scorched grease that I have breathed for fourteen years is gone instantly.

It is replaced by the sharp, chemical bite of rubbing alcohol and sterile sheets. I gasp, but my throat is completely blocked.

A thick, rigid plastic tube is shoved deep down my windpipe, forcing air into my lungs in rigid, mechanical bursts. Panic flares, raw and instinctive. My chest heaves against the ventilator.

I try to thrash, but my muscles are weak, practically unresponsive. My right hand twitches against the thin hospital mattress.

My fingers instinctively curl inward. I feel it. Pressed deep into my palm is the rough, worn cotton of a tiny woven sock.

The panic halts. The terror recedes, leaving only absolute clarity. The hallucination is over.

The doors are all broken. I am alive.

ALEX

The diesel engine roared, echoing through the Michigamee woods like a dying beast. Through the windshield, Vance saw him. The towering man in black, standing directly in his path, blocking the gate. Vance didn't hit the brakes. He didn't even attempt to swerve. His face twisted into a mask of pure, feral rage. He floored the gas pedal, the engine screaming as he intended to turn Alex into a smear on the frozen dirt and plow straight through him to get to Tyra.

The truck surged forward, closing the distance in seconds. Alex didn't flinch. He planted his boots firmly in the ice. He raised his right arm, leveling the large-caliber handgun, entirely ignoring the blinding glare of the headlights. He aimed low. Alex squeezed the trigger. Three deafening, rapid shots tore through the freezing air.

CHLOE

The frantic shrieking in the room grows louder, faster, matching the racing, terrified thumping of my own heart. The solid wooden door of the hospital room flies open.

Footsteps rush across the linoleum. A woman in dark blue scrubs appears over my bed, her eyes wide with shock. She reaches for the plastic tube in my throat, yelling over her shoulder down the bright hallway.

"I need a doctor in here! Bed four is awake!" The chaos erupts around me, but I don't care about the nurses or the alarms.

My neck is incredibly stiff, aching with a dull pain. I force my head to turn against the sterile pillow. I look past the IV poles and the glowing monitors.

I look for the one thing I need to see. I look for the broad, solid presence of my husband. I look for the man who promised me he would always keep the doors locked.

The vinyl visitor's chair next to my bed is completely empty. My breath catches against the plastic tube. The shield is gone.

ALEX

The bullets didn't hit the windshield. The first round shredded the thick rubber of the truck's front driver-side tire. The second and third rounds punched directly through the grill, shattering the radiator block. The tire blew out with a concussive blast that shook the frozen ground. The steel rim dropped, digging violently into the deep snow and dirt. The three-ton truck jerked to the left, completely out of Vance's control.

The machine skidded sideways across the ice, a sheer wall of rusted metal tearing toward Alex. He threw himself backward into the snow just as the rear bumper swung past, missing his head by inches. The truck careened off the dirt path. It slammed head-on into the trunk of a thick oak tree at the edge of the clearing. The impact sounded like a bomb going off.

The thick windshield instantly shattered into a million pieces. A thick, hissing cloud of white steam erupted from the dead radiator, swallowing the front of the cab. The truck's horn became stuck against the crushed steering wheel, blaring a continuous, dying wail into the freezing night.

Alex collapsed onto his knees in the snow. His arm dropped to his side. The slide of his handgun was locked back. It was completely empty. The truck was dead. But through the thick cloud of hissing steam, the driver's side door slowly, groaning violently against the crushed frame, began to open.

30 THE WRECKAGE

ALEX

The hissing of the ruptured radiator sounded like a nest of disturbed snakes. Thick, white steam poured from the crushed front end of the diesel truck, swallowing the freezing dirt clearing in a dense, blinding fog. The driver's side door groaned in protest. Metal shrieked against metal as a rugged boot kicked the crushed frame violently from the inside. The door snapped open.

Arthur Vance dropped heavily into the snow. He didn't look like a calculating predator anymore. He looked like a monster that had been backed into a corner and stripped of its skin. His face was a mask of dark, freezing blood from his shattered nose. His breath hitched in ragged, frantic gasps. He looked at the dead, smoking engine of his truck. He looked down the empty, dark logging road where the car had vanished. He had lost his daughter. He had lost his control.

Vance slowly turned his head toward the towering man kneeling in the snow. A low, guttural roar built in the back of Vance's throat—a sound of pure, unhinged, psychotic grief. He reached to his belt and drew the brutal, serrated hunting knife. Alex stared at him through the steam. He felt the cold seeping into his bones. His left arm hung dead at his side, the wool tourniquet soaked through. He raised his right hand, looked at the locked-back slide of his large-caliber handgun, and let it drop into the freezing mud.

He was out of bullets. He was out of strength. But the monster was still breathing, which meant the job wasn't done. Alex forced his battered body to stand. He planted his boots in the bloody snow, raised his one good fist, and waited for the charge.

CHLOE

The chaos in the ICU room is a blinding blur of blue scrubs and frantic voices. A doctor leans over me, his hands firm against my shoulders.

"Hold still, Chloe. I'm taking the tube out. Cough for me. Cough hard." I gag violently.

The rigid plastic tears at my raw throat as he pulls it free. I collapse back against the sterile pillows, gasping, pulling my first real, unassisted breath of air in what feels like a lifetime. It burns like fire.

"Vitals are stabilizing," a nurse calls out over the frantic beeping of the monitors. I ignore them.

I weakly lift my head, my eyes frantically searching the crowded room. My throat is so damaged I can barely force a sound out, but I have to know.

"Alex," I croak, the word scratching against my vocal cords like broken glass. "Where..." The solid wooden door to the hallway bursts open again.

A woman pushes her way past the nurses, her face pale and streaked with tears. It is Nina. Jason's wife.

She rushes to the side of my bed, completely ignoring the doctors. She grabs my left hand, gripping it with terrifying, trembling strength.

"Chloe," Nina sobs, her voice completely breaking. "Oh my god, you're awake."

"Where is he?" I whisper, the panic rising in my chest, choking me. The empty vinyl chair is mocking me. "Where is Alex?"

Nina shakes her head, the tears falling freely onto the sterile white sheets. "He found it," she whispers, her voice trembling with absolute terror. "He found the lockbox. He read the journal, Chloe. He knows about the compound. He knows about the baby."

My heart stops. The monitors beside me instantly spike.

"Jason tried to stop him," Nina cries, gripping my hand tighter. "But he wouldn't listen. He packed his guns, Chloe. He drove to Michigamee. He went to get your daughter back."

The stark, sterile walls of the hospital room seem to collapse inward. The air leaves my lungs.

Alex didn't leave me. He didn't abandon me to the dark. He read the darkest, most terrifying secret of my life, and instead of walking away, he picked up a gun and walked straight into my nightmare.

ALEX

Vance charged through the steam. The fight wasn't a tactical exchange. It was a desperate, ugly collision of two men with nothing left to lose. Vance swung the brutal, serrated blade in a wide, vicious arc. Alex ducked under the swing, driving his right shoulder directly into Vance's chest. The impact sent them both crashing into the twisted, sheared metal debris scattered around the front of the ruined truck.

Alex threw a crushing right hook, his knuckles connecting solidly with Vance's jaw. But Vance didn't feel it. Fueled by the unhinged frenzy of a father who had lost his child, Vance absorbed the blow and drove his knee directly into Alex's cracked ribs. Alex groaned, his vision flashing white with blinding agony. He stumbled backward against the crushed steel grill of the truck. It was the only opening Vance needed.

The monster lunged forward, driving all two hundred and fifty pounds of his weight behind the serrated hunting knife. The blade punched through the thick wool of Alex's sweater. It slid effortlessly between his ribs, burying itself deep into his abdomen until the cross guard slammed flush against his stomach. A shocking, agonizing cold erupted in Alex's core. His breath rushed out of his lungs in a ragged, bloody gasp. Vance stood inches away, his hands still gripping the handle of the knife, his blood-soaked face twisted into a victorious, psychotic sneer. He let go of the handle, preparing to step back and watch the imposing man fall.

Alex didn't fall. Instead of pushing the monster away, Alex let out a raw, guttural roar. He lunged forward, intentionally driving the blade even deeper into his own stomach to close the final inch of distance. Vance's eyes went wide with sudden, absolute shock. He was trapped in Alex's grip. Alex reached blindly behind him, his right hand gripping a foot-long, jagged shard of sheared steel ripped from the truck's shattered radiator.

Before Vance could break free, Alex drove the jagged steel spike violently forward. He didn't aim for the throat. He aimed for the shoulder. The jagged metal tore completely through the thick nylon of Vance's coat and the muscle of his collarbone. With a final, deafening roar of exertion, Alex drove his entire body weight forward, slamming Vance backward into the crushed, immovable steel frame of the truck's open door. The jagged spike punched completely through Vance and wedged itself deep into the twisted metal frame of the cab.

Vance let out a breathless, agonizing shriek. He instinctively reached up to pull the metal out, but his fingers slipped on the freezing blood. If he pulled the spike out, he would tear his own artery and bleed to death in seconds. If he left it in, he was entirely pinned to the solid steel door. He couldn't move. He couldn't chase. He was locked in place.

Alex stepped back, his legs finally giving out. He collapsed onto his knees in the freezing mud, clutching the handle of the knife still buried in his stomach. Vance thrashed against the twisted metal of the truck, his breath hitching in panicked, desperate gasps. For the first time in fourteen years, Arthur Vance looked out into the freezing, pitch-black woods, and realized he couldn't leave. He was in a cage, and the man with the key was dying in the snow.

Alex's chest heaved, his breaths becoming wet and shallow. He ignored the frantic struggles of the monster pinned to the wreckage. He looked past the truck, past the rusted padlock bunker, and out toward the dark, empty logging road. Tyra was out of the dark. Alex slowly lifted his head, looking up through the thick canopy of the pines. The winter clouds had cleared, revealing the cold, pale light of the North Star shining brilliantly against the dark sky. A faint, bloody smile touched the corners of his mouth. The war was over. He had kept his promise to his wife.

He had locked the doors. Alex closed his eyes, and let the quiet, thick snow cover him in the dark.

31 THE COST OF FREEDOM

JASON

The luxury sedan rolled to a stop beneath the glaring, artificial canopy of the hospital's emergency entrance in West Bloomfield. It was the middle of the night, but the sheer, blinding brightness of the city felt violently jarring after the absolute, suffocating darkness of the Michigamee woods. There were no howling winds here. No gunfire. Just the low hum of automatic doors and the distant wail of an ambulance siren.

Jason turned off the engine. His hands were still trembling, his knuckles white against the steering wheel. He had driven for seven straight hours in complete silence. He looked over at the passenger seat.

Tyra was curled into a tight ball, entirely swallowed by Alex's oversized, blood-stained black parka. She was shivering, shrinking away from the harsh fluorescent lights bleeding through the windshield. The reality of walking an undocumented, deeply traumatized fourteen-year-old girl into a modern medical facility hit Jason like a physical weight. There would be questions. There would be police.

But as he looked at the terrified girl wearing a brave man's coat, Jason knew he couldn't run this time. He had spent fourteen years hiding from the monster. The monster was dead, but the bill had finally come due.

"We're here," Jason whispered, his voice cracking. He unbuckled his seatbelt. "It's safe now. I'm going to take you to your mother."

CHLOE

The solid wooden door to my ICU room slowly pushes open. I am sitting up, ignoring the agonizing stiffness in my neck and the raw, burning pain in my throat.

I am waiting for the broad, solid frame of my husband to fill the doorway. I am waiting for Alex to walk in, bruised and bleeding, to tell me that the nightmare is finally over. But it isn't Alex.

Jason walks into the room alone. His expensive tailored overcoat is ruined, soaked with melted snow and dark stains. His face is pale, his eyes hollow and completely broken.

He stops at the foot of my bed. He doesn't look at Nina, who is standing tightly by my side. He looks directly at me, and the last shred of his carefully constructed facade entirely crumbles.

"I'm sorry," Jason whispers, the tears finally spilling over his eyelashes. "Chloe, I am so sorry."

"Where is he?" I ask, my voice a painful, raspy wheeze. "Jason, where is Alex?"

Jason shakes his head, his shoulders violently trembling. "I knew," he sobs, the confession tearing out of him. "Fourteen years ago, the night you escaped... I saw him, Chloe. I saw Artie in the alleyway."

"I knew he was alive. And I didn't tell you. I let you live in fear because I was a coward."

The heart monitor beside my bed begins to beep faster, matching the sudden, terrifying spike in my chest.

"Alex made me tell him everything," Jason cries, gripping the plastic rail at the foot of my bed. "I followed him, Chloe. After he left my house, I couldn't just sit there."

"I drove up after him... but I was too late to go into the woods. I just waited on the road until I saw her."

"Where is he?" I demand, gripping the sterile white sheets, the panic completely consuming me. Before Jason can answer, the solid wooden door opens again.

TYRA

The bright lights of the hallway burned her eyes. The floors were too smooth, the air too cold and smelling of sharp chemicals. Tyra dragged her rugged boots across the linoleum, clutching the oversized black parka tightly around her chest. The woman with the dark hair—Nina—was holding her shoulder gently, guiding her into a bright room filled with glowing, beeping machines. Tyra stepped nervously through the doorway.

There was a woman sitting in bed, entangled in wires and tubes. The woman's warm skin was drained of color, her face bruised and exhausted. Tyra stopped breathing.

The monster had always told her that the girl who climbed out the window was a liar. He had told her that her mother was a phantom who didn't care about her. But as Tyra looked at the woman in the bed, she saw the exact same dark eyes that stared back at her in the reflection of the rusted metal sink in the cage. She saw the exact same sharp jawline.

It wasn't a phantom. It was real.

CHLOE

The breath leaves my lungs entirely. The room, the beeping monitors, Jason's sobbing all completely vanishes. I am staring at a ghost.

She is so thin, so terrifyingly fragile, standing in the doorway like a frightened deer. But the face... the face is exactly the one I drew in my journal.

The dark eyes. The sharp jaw. It is the face I have seen in my nightmares for thousands of nights.

It is the infant I left in the dark, standing in the light. "Tyra," I whisper, the name tearing at my raw throat.

Tears flood my vision. The overwhelming, crushing weight of fourteen years of guilt collides violently with an impossible, miraculous relief. I force my battered body forward, reaching a trembling hand out toward the doorway.

Tyra takes a hesitant step closer. As she moves fully into the harsh hospital light, I finally see what she is wearing. She is entirely swallowed by a thick, black tactical parka.

My hand freezes in the air. I recognize the coat. It is Alex's.

But it is ruined. The collar and the thick nylon chest are soaked in dark, frozen blood. The blood freezes in my veins.

The empty vinyl visitor's chair next to my bed suddenly feels like a black hole, pulling all the air and light out of the room. I look frantically at Jason.

"Whose blood is that?" I beg, the terror ripping through my vocal cords. "Jason, whose blood is on that coat?"

TYRA

Tyra looked down at the dark, stiff stains on the thick nylon. She didn't look at the crying man at the foot of the bed. She looked directly at the woman with her eyes. She let go of the collar, her raspy, quiet voice cutting through the panic in the room.

"It's his," Tyra whispered.

The woman in the bed stopped struggling. She stared at Tyra, completely paralyzed.

"The towering man," Tyra said, her voice shaking as she remembered the absolute dark of the woods. "The monster was coming for me. The formidable man stepped in front of the gun. He bled for me."

Tyra reached up and touched the fabric of the coat. It still smelled faintly of the cold and the pine trees.

"He took off his armor and gave it to me," Tyra whispered, the tears finally welling in her dark eyes. "He told me to put the star at my back and run. He told me he was going to go back into the dark... to lock the doors."

The woman in the bed let out a sound that Tyra would never forget. It wasn't a scream. It was a raw, devastating shatter of a soul breaking entirely in half. The woman collapsed forward, burying her face in her hands as she wept, her agonizing sobs filling the sterile room. Tyra stood in the bright light, wrapped in the brave man's armor, and realized that her freedom had been bought with everything this woman had left to love.

BACK MATTER

32 THE LIGHT (EPILOGUE)

CHLOE

One Year Later

The wind coming off the lake is sharp and cold, but it doesn't smell like damp earth or scorched grease. It smells like pine needles and fresh, open water.

I stand on the wooden deck of the small A-frame cabin we rented in Traverse City. I wrap my cardigan tighter around my shoulders, letting the morning sun warm my face. I don't close my eyes. I want to see every inch of the horizon.

I turn my head, looking through the sliding glass door into the kitchen. Tyra is standing at the counter.

She is taller now, the terrifying, hollowed-out frailty of the cage slowly giving way to the strength of a fifteen-year-old girl. She is making tea, her movements are quiet and deliberate.

She pauses, looking out the kitchen window at the vast, open expanse of the water. She doesn't flinch at the sudden cry of a seagull.

She doesn't shrink away from the blinding reflection of the sun on the waves. She is still quiet, and there are still nights when she wakes up terrified, but she isn't hiding in the dark anymore.

She turns, catching me watching her. The sharp line of her jaw softens. She offers a small, fragile smile.

I smile back, the familiar ache blooming in my chest. The grief is still there. It will always be there.

But it isn't the suffocating, toxic guilt that kept me locked in a hallway of doors for fourteen years. It is a clean, honest grief. It is the price of the life I am standing in right now.

Tyra picks up her mug and walks out onto the deck. She isn't wearing the oversized, blood-stained black parka anymore. We cleaned it, folded it, and placed it in a cedar chest at the foot of her bed.

It is her armor, but she doesn't need to wear it every day to feel safe. She stands next to me, leaning her elbows against the wooden railing.

"It's bright today," she says, her voice still holding that raspy edge, but no longer a terrified whisper.

"It is," I reply softly, reaching out to rest my hand over hers. We stand together in silence, looking out over the water.

My right hand instinctively traces the shape of the tiny, yellowed cotton infant's sock I keep tucked into the pocket of my cardigan. The anchor.

I look up at the clear, infinite blue sky. There is no steel ceiling. There are no rusted padlocks.

I think of the imposing man who walked into the freezing dark so we could stand in the sun. I think of the man who traded his final breath to dismantle my nightmare.

He didn't just save my daughter; he saved me from the ghost I had been fighting my entire life. I take a deep, clear breath of the freezing air.

"Are you ready to go inside?" I ask Tyra, a gentle breeze pulling at her dark hair.

Tyra looks at the cabin door. She nods slowly, her dark eyes reflecting the morning light. "Yeah. I'm ready."

We turn our backs to the wind and walk back into the warmth of the house. I reach out, slide the glass door shut behind us, and leave it completely unlocked.

THE CALL TO ACTION

Thank You for Reading

I hope you enjoyed the dark, gripping journey of Chloe and Alex in **A Grieving Embrace: The Cage She Left Behind**.

As an independent creator, I don't rely on massive traditional publishing marketing budgets to get this story into the hands of readers. I rely entirely on readers like you.

If this story kept you turning the pages late into the night, the single greatest compliment you can give is to leave a brief, honest review on Amazon, Goodreads, or wherever you purchased this book. Even just a rating and one sentence about your favorite character or plot twist makes a massive difference in helping other thriller fans discover the Michigamee woods.

What's Next?

The story doesn't end on the page. *A Grieving Embrace* is currently being developed for the screen.

To get the audiobook, exclusive updates on the upcoming film adaptation, and the official music soundtrack connect with me online: https://beacons.ai/tvsnowdenjr

Thank you for stepping into the dark with me.

— Tyrece V. Snowden Jr.